"I know you must have been pretty angry with me when I left the way I did."

"Buck, that was twenty years ago," Ellie reminded him gently, her tone carefully neutral. Why did he want to dig up the past, when there was so much to deal with right now in the present?

"Still," he drawled slowly, "you must want to know what happened back then."

Ellie shrugged. "If you want to tell me, I'll listen."

Buck stepped back, looking stunned as if she'd slapped his face. "It didn't matter to you that I left?"

Ellie frowned. "Of course it mattered. A lot of people in this town thought—I thought—you and I had a future together."

Buck was silent, and Ellie wondered what he was thinking about. He shook his head but didn't speak.

Books by Deb Kastner

Love Inspired

A Holiday Prayer
Daddy's Home
Black Hills Bride
The Forgiving Heart
A Daddy at Heart
A Perfect Match
The Christmas Groom
Hart's Harbor
Undercover Blessings
The Heart of a Man
A Wedding in Wyoming
His Texas Bride

DEB KASTNER

lives and writes in colorful Colorado with the front range of the Rocky Mountains for inspiration. She loves writing for the Steeple Hill Love Inspired line, where she can write about her two favorite things—faith and love. Her characters range from upbeat and humorous to (her favorite) dark and broody heroes. Her plots fall anywhere in between, from a playful romp to the deeply emotional.

Deb's books have been twice nominated for the *RT Book Reviews* Reviewers' Choice Award for Best Inspirational Novel of the Year.

Deb and her husband share their home with their two youngest daughters. Deb is thrilled about the newest member of the family—her first granddaughter, Isabella. What fun to be a granny!

Deb loves to hear from her readers. You can contact her by e-mail at DEBWRTR@aol.com, or on her MySpace or Facebook pages.

His Texas Bride
Deb Kastner

Steeple
Hill®

Published by Steeple Hill Books™

STEEPLE HILL BOOKS

Steeple
Hill®

Recycling programs
for this product may
not exist in your area.

ISBN-13: 978-0-373-87587-0

HIS TEXAS BRIDE

www.SteepleHill.com

Printed in U.S.A.

Therefore if you bring your gift to the altar, and there remember that your brother has something against you, leave your gift there before the altar, and go your way. First be reconciled to your brother, and then come and offer your gift.

—*Matthew* 5:23, 24

All my love to my dearest daughter Kimberly.
Your strength and courage inspire me.

Chapter One

Mama loved carnations.

Buck Redmond gently laid the small, sweetly pungent bouquet of purple and yellow carnations against the headstone carved with his mother's initials, careful not to disturb the freshly turned earth that framed the graveside. He brushed his suddenly tear-stung eyes with his thumb and forefinger and, for the hundredth time that morning, wished he'd come home even a day sooner.

He'd never planned to return home at all. But for his mother's funeral, he'd had no choice. Despite the rift he'd created between them, Buck loved his mother, and now he'd never be able to tell her just how much.

But there was no use thinking about things that could never be. Buck had learned that the hard way. He'd make arrangements to sell his mother's property and get out of town as fast as he'd had to return. His childhood home, once a horse ranch and now Esther's House of Crafts, held few good memories for him, anyway.

Buck stood and replaced his black Stetson on his

head. Then, feeling like he should say a prayer for his mother but not knowing how, he turned away.

Right into the arms of Ellie McBride.

Ellie.

The last person on earth he wanted to see right now.

"I thought I'd find you here," she said softly, placing her palms on his elbows as if to balance him.

Buck took an unconscious step backward. If he was going to fall down—and he wasn't—a small, raven-haired wisp of a woman like Ellie wouldn't have been able to keep him vertical. Besides, he still felt that little zap of electricity whenever she touched him. It hadn't gone away, not in twenty years.

He was thirty-eight years old now, not an awkward teenager anymore. He and Ellie had both moved on with their lives. He pulled the brim of his hat down low over his eyes.

"What do you want?" he asked. His words came out a bit more gruffly than he'd intended, but he didn't apologize.

"I've been looking for you," she said simply.

"Why?"

"I'm holding a reception for your mother's passing at my...." She hesitated, stumbling over her words.

Buck wondered why, but he didn't ask. He had no intention of going to any reception in this town, but telling Ellie that without hurting her feelings was another thing entirely.

"At...at my ranch house," she concluded, gushing out the words. "The whole town is there, Buck. They want to pay their respects to you—and your son. Where is Tyler, anyway?"

That was exactly what Buck was afraid of, the whole town being there, especially where his son, Tyler, was concerned. He would have left twelve-year-old Tyler with someone—anyone—if there *was* anyone to leave him with, which there wasn't.

"Tyler is waiting in my truck," he said, choosing to answer the obvious and avoid the rest for as long as he could.

"Oh, good. I didn't get the chance to meet him at the funeral," she said, her voice husky as she tried for a light tone but didn't quite succeed.

Ellie reached out and touched Buck's arm again, this time sliding her hand down his forearm to reach for his palm. Buck had forgotten how tiny her hand felt in his, and he simply stared at their hands as their fingers met.

"I couldn't even get close to you," she said softly. "You took off right after the funeral this morning without a word to anyone."

That much was true. He simply nodded, unable to speak for the well of emotion in his throat.

"I wanted to tell you and Tyler how sorry I am about the loss of Esther," she continued in her high, lilting voice, unashamed of the tears that coursed down her cheeks. "You know your mother was always like a second mom to me. I will miss her desperately. I can't imagine how you feel."

Actually, Ellie could imagine just that, Buck thought, if anyone could. Ellie *had* been close to his mother, ever since Buck and Ellie had first started dating in his junior—her sophomore—year of high school. Ellie's own mother had died when she was a small child. Perhaps that was the reason Buck's mother and Ellie had formed such a strong, loving bond.

And maybe that was what made it so much harder to imagine returning home at all.

Buck didn't really want to think about that right now. He pulled his fingers from her grasp. "I appreciate the sentiment," he said roughly, his throat closing around the words, "and I'm sure you went to a lot of trouble for the reception, so I'm sorry to say Tyler and I won't be able to make it."

He wasn't sorry, but it seemed like the polite thing to say. But in his years away from Ellie McBride, he'd apparently forgotten one of her more annoying qualities—her stubborn nature.

"Of course you're going to the reception," she replied in a no-nonsense voice that brooked no argument. "Buck, your mother just passed. You may not care about the people in this town, but they care about you."

Ellie glared at him, daring him to argue with her. When he didn't speak, she continued her tirade as if she hadn't even paused. "And they cared about your mother. It would be good of you to allow them to express their grief at her loss."

"I don't owe the people in this town a thing," he bit out, shaking his head.

He believed his own words. The town he'd been born and raised in had betrayed his trust in everything he'd believed in. They'd sold their souls to the almighty dollar.

Ellie.

Even his own mother.

Why should he care what the town folks of Ferrell thought about him? He should get out of town right now, while the getting was good.

"Larry Bowman is there," Ellie went on, obviously ignoring the fact that Buck had pulled away from her yet again. "I'm sure he'd be willing to talk with you about your mother's will as soon as the reception is finished."

Buck groaned aloud. With grief shrouding his thoughts, he'd temporarily forgotten he would have to take care of his mother's estate before leaving town. He wanted to leave *now*. Grief washed through him once again, shadowing his other feelings.

He was his mother's only child, and no doubt the sole beneficiary of her will. He needed to speak with Larry Bowman, the town lawyer, sooner or later; at the moment, his heart was voting for later rather than sooner.

"I don't know if I can do that," he said, his voice gruff and low. He pinched his lips together. He hadn't meant to say the words aloud.

"I can't imagine what you're going through," Ellie said in an equally low tone, repeating her earlier sentiment. "I know this is a rough time for you. If it helps, I'll be at the reading of the will."

Buck's head jerked up, and he looked Ellie straight in her deep violet eyes for the first time. He was thoroughly shaken by the amount of warmth and compassion he read there—he'd expected more anger, he supposed—but even so, it was her words that unsettled him the most.

"Why would you be there?"

Ellie shook her head, looking away from his gaze and squeezing her eyes closed for a brief moment.

Buck wondered if she had something to hide—something she wasn't telling him. Not that he would ask.

"I just know I've been asked to attend," she said, opening her eyes and once more making eye contact with him. "And I thought it might help if you had a— a *friend*," she stammered awkwardly, "by your side through all this."

Buck turned away, unable to meet her gaze any longer. Ellie had been a friend, the best friend he'd ever had. But she had been so much more than that.

His first love.

Puppy love, some might have called it, but Buck knew better in his heart.

Ellie McBride had been his first love—if he were completely honest with himself, his only love.

But that was a long time ago, in another lifetime. Too much had happened since then, for them both. He was amazed she would still consider herself to be anything to him, much less call herself his friend.

At long last he sighed and turned back to her. "All right," he said, surrendering to the inevitable. "I'll go to your reception. But I'm not sure what to do with Tyler. He doesn't want to be here at all. I don't think he'll be keen on meeting the folks of Ferrell, Texas. Especially right now."

Ellie nodded, her beautiful violet eyes gleaming. "I understand. I wouldn't want to be around a bunch of strangers if I were grieving for my beloved grandmother, either. And twelve is a tough age for a boy."

Buck barely held back his disbelief. What would she know about twelve-year-old boys? Buck's mother, on her brief visits to see Buck and Tyler on the west side of Texas, had mentioned more than once that Ellie had never married—not that he had asked. But he knew why his mother had persisted in bringing the subject up: always in the hope he would return to Ferrell, something he'd long since vowed never to do.

Until now.

"Listen, I think I can handle Tyler," Ellie said, brushing her long, thick, straight black hair back from her forehead with her thumb and middle finger. "Why don't we head over to the ranch, and I'll see what I can do?"

Buck knew any overtures to Tyler on Ellie's part would be met with resistance by his surly son. Tyler was a handful, with a chip on his shoulder the size of Texas itself.

But what else could Buck do?

He nodded and gestured toward the church, where he'd parked his truck. They walked in silence, Ellie obviously lost in her own thoughts and Buck wondering what she was thinking. Maybe he didn't want to know.

Ellie had enough reason to hate Buck for what he'd done to her twenty years ago. For all they'd meant to each other, he'd disappeared out of her life without a single word to her.

Her compassion in light of their past together confused him. Perhaps she was doing this only for the sake of his mother. He sensed an unseen wall between them, erected by Ellie's emotions, one he knew he couldn't break down even if he wanted to. He'd built that wall with his own two hands.

Not that it mattered, he told himself.

Buck knocked on the glass on the passenger's side of his pickup truck, a vehicle that had seen better days.

Tyler, dressed in a new pair of blue jeans and a blue denim shirt, had his head back against the seat and his eyes closed, his MP3 player in his hand and earphones in his ears. Buck knew Tyler wasn't dozing, even when he didn't so much as open an eyelid to Buck's persistent knocking.

Maybe the boy was playing his music too loud to hear Buck knocking.

Choosing to give Tyler the benefit of the doubt, Buck dug his keys from the front left pocket of his black jeans, unlocked the door and opened it.

"Wake up, kiddo," he gently told his son, shaking the boy by the shoulder. He presumed Tyler was intentionally ignoring him, as he had been all through the trip back to Ferrell, and through the funeral service, as well. "I want to introduce you to someone."

That got the boy's attention. Apparently Tyler's music wasn't as loud as Buck had first supposed.

Tyler opened his eyes—blue, like his mother's—and scrubbed a hand through his light blond hair, also a maternal trait, not at all like Buck's own sandy brown hair and green eyes.

Ellie stepped forward, extending her hand. "Hi, Tyler. It's nice to meet you. I'm Ellie McBride. I was a friend of your grandmother. And your father," she said, making it sound almost like an afterthought. "I'm truly sorry for your loss."

Tyler squinted down at Ellie's outstretched hand but ignored it. Instead, he simply shrugged and tipped his head back against the seat, closing his eyes once again.

"Miss McBride is having a reception in honor of your grandmother," Buck said sternly, wishing he'd taught his son better manners, though glancing at Ellie, she didn't seem to have taken the least offense at Tyler's breach of etiquette. She was smiling compassionately at the boy.

"There are quite a few boys your age," she offered. "I can introduce you, if you'd like. Maybe you can make a few new friends while you're in town."

Tyler grunted and shook his head, and Buck began to think he'd raised a Neanderthal. How could he blame the boy, though? Buck knew all about being silent and broody. He'd invented it.

"Tyler, get out of the truck. Now," he stated in a firm, no-nonsense voice.

"No," Tyler and Ellie replied at the same time.

Buck didn't know who to glare at first, so he swept his gaze across both of them.

"Really, there's no need," Ellie continued. At least she was attempting to explain herself, while Buck's own son chose to ignore him completely. "My ranch is just north of town, just off Main Street, to the right. McBride's Christian Therapy Ranch. You can't miss the sign."

Therapy ranch?

That was a mighty fancy name for a tourist trap, Buck thought with an internal scoff. He wanted to cringe in distaste. This was exactly why he'd left Ferrell in the first place.

Instead, he kept his thoughts to himself. Forcing himself to be polite, he tipped his hat at Ellie and strode purposefully to the driver's side of the truck. "We'll see you there."

* * *

Ellie's meeting with Buck and Tyler hadn't gone at all as she'd anticipated. Actually, she'd had no idea what to expect—not after twenty years.

What she *hadn't* expected was how quickly all her feelings came back, flooding into her heart as if someone had opened a gate. Buck still made her stomach weak with butterflies and her heart sing, no matter how she tried to tamp it down.

Frankly, Ellie hadn't expected to feel anything for Buck. Twenty years was a long time.

And if she felt anything, it should be anger, she mused. But she'd buried that emotion ages ago, and it hadn't returned, at least not yet. Not even when she'd first seen Buck at his mother's graveside. God's forgiveness was an amazing thing—she knew it wasn't her own spirit that had healed her heart.

Time had healed her heart. That, and a lot of prayer. Still, she continued to surprise herself. Ellie had felt a bit of righteous indignation on Buck's mother's behalf, perhaps, but not what she would classify as anger.

And as she watched Buck now, standing in the middle of her family room, surrounded by townspeople he'd known all his life, she felt nothing but pity. Buck had once been the most important part of her world. She had moved on, but Buck, Buck looked like a man who'd seen one too many days on the rough side of life.

At least he looked more comfortable now than he had at the graveside, having shed his Western jacket and bolo tie. He was still dressed entirely in black, however. His Western shirt was now open at the collar, although, she mused with a touch of amusement, Buck still looked a little like he was choking.

It was probably the crowd suffocating him, Ellie thought. One more painful reminder of how much he'd changed. She remembered a time in his high school years when Buck had once loved being the center of attention.

Speaking of attention, Ellie realized she hadn't seen Tyler enter her dwelling with Buck. She felt an instinctive kinship and a sense of responsibility to the boy, who, under different circumstances, might have been her own son.

He wasn't, but that didn't stop Ellie from a small burst of maternal feeling. Of course, Tyler didn't want to spend an afternoon surrounded by people he didn't know offering him condolences on his grandmother's passing.

Buck's mother, whom Ellie had called Mama Esther for as long as she could remember, had been especially close to Tyler. Ellie knew from Mama Esther's recounting how difficult a time Tyler had had adjusting to his mother's abandonment when he was only two years old.

And now, at age twelve, poor Tyler had lost his beloved grandmother.

Ellie excused herself from her hostess duties and slipped into the homey, aromatic kitchen and out the back door. Pausing for a moment to push her hair out of her face, she made her way to the front of the house, where Buck's truck was parked amid the rest of the town's vehicles.

Cupping her hand over her forehead against the sun's incessant glare, she peeked inside the window, hoping to catch a glimpse of Tyler.

The truck was empty.

Ellie was surprised. She'd been certain she'd find the young man locked in the truck with his MP3 player blasting in his ears, as he'd been earlier. It was what she would have done were she the one in Tyler's place.

But, she realized with sudden insight, it wasn't what *Buck* would have done given the same circumstances. And suddenly she knew exactly where to look for Tyler.

Turning on her heel, she strode away from the truck, but not the way she'd come. Not back to the house. Instead, she turned down the trail to her stable.

Somehow, in the deepest part of her heart, she was certain she'd find Tyler there.

Buck looked around for Ellie, but she had disappeared. He admitted to being a little surprised, actually, when he'd entered Ellie's ranch house and had seen all the people milling around, eating and chatting.

Every word Ellie had said was true.

The whole town *was* there, and his old friends and neighbors had quickly surrounded him to voice their condolences over the loss of his mother. Buck had known his mother was well loved in Ferrell, but he believed himself to be as equally—and understandably—despised and couldn't have imagined the magnitude of compassion and acceptance he was experiencing with people he'd long since put out of his heart and his life.

He'd clearly underestimated them. All of them. It occurred to him that this might have been the case all along.

Whatever changes had happened in Ferrell, it was

obviously still a small town at heart. People here really cared. He hadn't given them enough credit for that. He'd thought they'd turn fancy and snobbish once the highway was built and tourist money started lining their pockets.

That he was wrong surprised and discomfited him.

And the food!

Everyone had brought their best dishes to share for the occasion. Buck was used to bunkhouse fare, and the layout of food here at Ellie's was better than at any of the church potlucks he remembered attending as a child here in Ferrell. His stomach was soon as heavy as his heart was light.

It seemed only minutes had passed when Larry Bowman clapped Buck on the back of his shoulder. "The crowd is starting to disperse," he said in a kind, gentle tone. Larry had been the town lawyer for as long as Buck could remember. "We can get down to business anytime you're ready."

"Sure," Buck choked out, struggling for a breath. Why did he feel like he was being ambushed? Try as he might, he couldn't shake it. "Just give me a few minutes, will you? I need to check on my son."

Larry nodded in agreement and quickly moved back toward the nearest group of neighbors, giving Buck the space he so desperately needed.

Find his son?

What Buck needed to do was find *Ellie*. He realized he hadn't seen her in an hour.

Ellie was a social being. Buck had expected her to be flitting around like a butterfly as hostess of this party, or at least that was how she'd been twenty years ago. He realized, with a pang of some emotion he refused to identify, that he really knew nothing of the woman she'd become.

Despite that fact, though, he had a less-than-altruistic reason for finding Ellie—the reading of the will. His tough veneer was a sham, and he knew it. And if he wasn't careful, everyone else would know it, as well.

Where was she?

Buck asked around, but no one had seen her in a while. And then Buck remembered something Ellie had said earlier, when they were at the gravesite together. She'd said she would handle Tyler, once they'd agreed to come to the reception at her ranch.

Was that where she was?

With Tyler?

Ellie was in for trouble if she had any notion of pulling Tyler out of his shell. The boy was so angry and bitter, he rarely talked to Buck anymore, much less some strange woman from a town his father rarely spoke of, and only then with an animosity he knew he could not hide. He wouldn't be too keen on anything Ellie offered, especially meeting new friends. Tyler had always been a bit of a loner.

Like Buck.

Even so, Buck's gut was telling him he was on the right track with that line of reasoning, that he would find Tyler wherever Ellie was lurking.

Ellie had always been a stubborn woman, and Buck doubted that had changed in twenty years. She would be a formidable opponent, even for Tyler, though Buck wasn't the least bit certain who would win any quarrel between them.

Buck hoped there was no quarrel.

Spinning on his heels, he clamped his black Stetson down on his head and moved slowly and awkwardly toward the front door, having to explain several times that, no, he was not leaving so soon, but rather that he was trying to find his son so he could introduce Tyler around.

If Buck could get the boy out of the truck. And if Ellie's feelings weren't too hurt by his son's sharp tongue and broody disposition.

The scenario in Buck's mind was looking worse by the minute. Tyler biting into Ellie in suppressed grief over the death of his beloved grandmother. Ellie forcing Tyler to meet kids his own age, when all that would do was make the boy even more uncomfortable than he already was. Buck couldn't get to his truck fast enough—only to find it empty when he arrived.

Chapter Two

Ellie's theory had been right on the mark. Once she'd remembered whose son Tyler was, she'd known just where to look for him—in the stable, with the horses.

Where Buck would have hidden given the same set of circumstances.

The boy obviously shared the same love for horses as his father, because as soon as Ellie entered the stable, she knew Tyler was present. She could hear Tyler making the same soft crooning sounds his father had always used—quite effectively, she clearly remembered—with his own horses.

"Tyler?" she called cheerfully, but her only answer was a sudden deafening silence in the stable. "Tyler Redmond? It's Ellie McBride. We met earlier."

Still no sound, but Ellie was no less certain Tyler was somewhere in the stable, and that he was no doubt straining his ears for any sound she might make. She moved noisily from stall to stall, speaking to each of her beloved horses as she went and thus giving Tyler plenty of warning—wherever he was. It was only when she peeked over the last door, the one to the birthing stall, that she found Tyler.

One of her quarter horse broodmares, Sophie, was due to deliver soon, so the sorrel-colored mare had been recently confined to the roomy birthing stall, filled with fresh straw to welcome the newborn foal whenever he or she came. Ellie thought it would be soon.

To Ellie's alarm, Sophie was lying on her side, her breath coming in heaving snorts. Tyler was there with the sorrel, on his knees, hunkered over the mare, rubbing her down with his own bandana and murmuring encouragement to her. Ellie noted vaguely that Tyler's denim shirt was now untucked, and the boy had obviously given no thought to dirtying his crisp new blue jeans as he knelt before the laboring mare.

"Tyler?" Ellie said again. "What is it? What's wrong with Sophie?"

She realized belatedly she had no idea why she was asking a twelve-year-old boy such a question, but she opened the stall door and slipped inside, sliding to her knees next to the horse's head and running her hand down Sophie's sweat-stained withers, then rapidly across her stomach, mentally assessing how far into labor Sophie might be.

Her adrenaline surged as she realized help for the birth was not readily available. Doc Stevens, the local vet, wasn't inside the ranch house with the rest of the community. Just after Esther's funeral, the vet had been unexpectedly called away for an emergency at a nearby farm.

Ellie toyed with the idea of having Tyler run and ask

someone at the house to fetch Doc Stevens immediately. Still, she waited patiently for the boy's answer to her query, allowing Tyler the opportunity to voice his own opinion, as he'd been with the mare longer.

Tyler looked up at her with the same serious, low-browed gaze Buck often wore, shadowed by a camel-colored felt cowboy hat pushed low over his eyes. The boy reminded Ellie of his father in so many ways, it made her heart turn over and emotions clog in her throat.

"She's in labor," Tyler said, his voice at once soft and gruff, with the high-pitched twinge of a young man entering puberty. "It's been an hour, maybe?"

Ellie smiled inwardly. She might have pointed out that she had already assessed that much just by looking at the situation, but she didn't. Instead, she nodded briskly and allowed the boy to continue. "And?"

"Well, I found her this way," Tyler explained, shrugging his shoulders. "I know mares lie down to give birth, but it seems to me she's struggling awfully hard. I think the foal might be in the wrong position."

That was exactly what Ellie was thinking. She smiled encouragement to the boy and then frowned as she thought through the implications of this situation. "Our town vet couldn't make it to the reception," she explained hastily. "Some kind of emergency at a neighboring ranch. I may need you to find your dad and have him drive you out to find Doc Stevens, the vet."

The boy scowled for a moment, then nodded briskly. Obviously the idea of dashing into a house of strangers to find his dad was not high on Tyler's list of things to do, much less jaunt all over town, looking for a veterinarian he didn't even know.

The boy surprised her. Despite his obvious discomfort, Tyler tipped his cowboy hat with his fingers and answered her politely, if not willingly. "Yes, ma'am," he replied.

At that moment the mare made a horrible groaning sound, almost a scream. Ellie and Tyler at once turned their attention back to Sophie. Ellie had been breeding horses long enough to realize that Sophie shouldn't be experiencing the kind of pain she was obviously in. As Tyler had gravely noted, something was definitely wrong.

A gush of liquid from the mare sealed it for Ellie. There wasn't time to go for help. "I've changed my mind, Tyler. I need you with me. Do you think you can give me a hand? Sophie is obviously delivering this foal *now.*"

"Yes, ma'am," Tyler answered, his brilliant blue eyes shining delightedly at this new opportunity. Once again Tyler reminded Ellie of his father. Ellie was surprised at the quiet respect the young man showed her. He'd appeared so bitter and broody earlier. But like his father, Ellie guessed, Tyler had a special bond with horses—apparently enough of a connection to allow the boy to set his other concerns aside.

"There is a box of supplies in the corner. I need you to grab the tape and wrap Sophie's tail for me."

Without a word, Tyler went to work, efficiently wrapping the mare's tail while Ellie held it up for him.

"You've done this before," Ellie stated.

"Yes, ma'am. A few times."

"Good. I can use your experience."

Tyler looked up at her, surprise—and maybe a little pride—evident in his expression. One corner of his mouth tipped up ever so slightly. Ellie thought that might be the closest thing to a smile she'd seen from the boy.

"Now what?" he asked softly. "Dad and I usually let our mares do the work themselves."

Ellie nodded. "And that's what we'll do, as well. This isn't Sophie's first foal, so she knows what she's doing. We'll just stand back and watch God's miracle of birth. Hopefully that's all it will take and Sophie will manage this just fine on her own, but just in case, we'd better stick around and be ready to lend a hand if it becomes necessary."

Tyler moved to the side of the stall and leaned a somewhat brawny shoulder against the wall. He maintained some of the gangly awkwardness of puberty, but he was a handsome boy, Ellie thought—just as his father had been. Clearly farm life kept Tyler in good physical shape. He looked a good deal stronger than most boys his age. Ellie remembered that Buck had been much the same way at age twelve.

She remembered far more about Buck Redmond than she ought to, she thought, frowning inwardly. She had let that part of her life go—at least she thought she had, until he'd shown up again, twenty years later.

Hopefully, Ellie thought, she was twenty years *wiser.*

As for her heart, well, she couldn't vouch for that.

"Look!" Tyler exclaimed, moving to hunch beside the mare. "I can see the foal's legs!"

Ellie leaned over Tyler to view the foal's progress.

She, too, saw the legs, which normally appeared first. But she immediately recognized the problem.

"It's a breech birth," she explained to Tyler as she bent in to take a closer look. "See, the hooves are pointed upward, toward the top of the mare. With a normal birth the hooves point down."

Tyler frowned. "I've never seen a breech birth," he admitted. "What does that mean? Should I run and fetch the vet now?" His voice was a mixture of alarm and concern.

Ellie was pleased that the young boy was suddenly so willing to do a task he had not been so eager to perform earlier, but she shook her head. "No need. Breech births don't generally require a vet's presence. Let's just wait and see what happens."

The boy nodded, his gaze full of compassion as he shifted slightly so he could run his hand down the mare's withers. "Easy there, girl," he murmured in the same rich tone his father used with horses.

Ellie smiled softly. Tyler *was* like his father in so many ways, not just physically. She wished, with a moment's flash of melancholy, she could see Tyler grow up. But that was not meant to be, and there was no use brooding about it.

The unlikely pair, Ellie and Tyler, waited patiently while the horse strained to birth her foal. After several silent minutes, Ellie knelt down by the mare, on the opposite side of Tyler.

"I think she's going to need a little help," she said softly so as not to disturb Sophie.

"Yeah?" Tyler still sounded concerned for the animal, but there was now excitement in his voice, as well.

"Yes," Ellie agreed, smiling at Tyler. "And I'm glad I have a strong young man like you here to help me. We need to put a little pressure on the foal's legs."

Tyler's eyes were bright for a moment, and then he frowned. "How do you mean?"

Ellie threw him a towel, which he absently tossed across his shoulder.

"Use the towel to get a good grip on the foal's legs," she instructed him. "Then gently pull them upward, toward the mare's back."

Tyler didn't speak as he followed Ellie's instructions. Sweat broke out on his brow as he gritted his teeth and strained to dislodge the backward-facing foal.

"You're doing a perfect job, son," Ellie encouraged as the foal's legs, still covered by a thick membrane, became more visible. "The hips are the hardest part of a breech birth. As you apply pressure, you're helping Sophie get the foal in the right position to deliver as easily as possible."

Tyler pinched his lips together in the shadow of a smile. "Yes, ma'am. I can feel the movement. I think she—"

The young man didn't finish his sentence as the back half of the foal slid from his mother, followed quickly by the head. Tyler whooped in excitement. "Good going, Sophie."

Ellie broke the sac around the foal's head and then stood up and took a couple steps backward. "It's time to let Sophie take over," she told Tyler.

Tyler grinned, really grinned, this time. "I've seen this part before. Never get tired of it, though." His voice was full of excitement and pride.

"Can you tell if it's a boy or a girl?" Ellie asked, her own excitement and pride washing through her as she watched the gentle miracle of a mare tending her newborn foal.

Tyler, who had also risen to his feet, leaned over the foal, then took off his tan felt cowboy hat and clapped it against his thigh. "It's a boy, ma'am. You have a fine colt here."

"Thank God for a healthy birth," Ellie whispered and then paused, considering her words carefully. "You know, I'm so glad you were here with me today. I couldn't have made it without you, Tyler. Sophie and I appreciate what you did."

Tyler's face flushed with color, and he returned his hat to his head, low over his eyes, just as his father wore *his* hat most of the time.

"Yes, ma'am," was all he said, but despite Tyler's attempt to shade his features with his hat, Ellie saw a glimpse of his gleaming blue eyes, bright with pride and joy.

"Tyler James Redmond, just what do you think you're doing out here?"

Buck's voice obviously startled the boy, making Tyler jump from where he'd been crouching in the stable, staring down at something Buck couldn't see from his vantage point.

"He was helping me," came Ellie's voice from behind Buck, making *him* jump. Just like a woman to sneak up on a man. Buck whirled around to face her, lifting one eyebrow as he stared down into her gorgeous face. Time had been good to Ellie. She looked

just as stunning as she had when she was seventeen—
even more beautiful, if that were possible.

"If you'd take a good look over the stable door,
you'd see *what,*" she said, sounding annoyed. "Tyler
and I have been busy."

Ellie made it sound like she and his son were old
friends, and Tyler was beaming back at Ellie as if the
sun rose and set at her presence.

What had she done to his boy?

This was the same sulky teenager who refused to
utter two sentences straight to his own father and
never, ever smiled, at least that Buck could remember.
Tyler's constant scowl was a mirror of Buck's own
image, he knew.

But this was something different.

Way different.

Ellie opened the stall door and gestured for Buck to
go inside ahead of her. Tyler's smile changed to a scowl
as Buck strode in, but Buck ignored it for the moment.
Buck removed his hat and tucked it under his arm.

"So what's the story?" he asked gruffly. As soon as
the words were out of his mouth, he saw the answer to
his own question wriggling on the soft straw of the
stall floor.

"Your son just delivered a foal," Ellie said, sounding
as proud as if she were speaking of her own child. "A
breech birth. You should be proud of him, Buck."

Buck *was* proud, but he'd never known how to
express it, so he just shrugged.

Tyler stared at Buck for a long moment, his eyes
narrowing with each second, until finally he muttered
something under his breath and turned away.

"What did you say?" Buck demanded of his son.

"If you heard me, why do you have to ask?" Tyler replied sarcastically, then strode from the stall and out the stable door before Buck could say another word.

Buck looked at Ellie, who was staring at him as if he'd grown a third arm. "What did I say?" he queried defensively.

Ellie vehemently shook her head. "This was a special moment for Tyler, Buck," she snapped, staring off the way Tyler had gone. "The least you could have done would have been to say something nice, something to let him know you are proud of your only son. Was that too much to ask?"

"Give me a break, Ellie. I was caught off guard. I couldn't think of anything to tell the boy. You know I'm not good at saying things out loud."

Ellie scoffed. "*That* I do remember."

Buck had the distinct impression the subject had changed, though he'd always had difficulty following the train of a woman's thoughts—especially Ellie McBride's.

But he wasn't that oblivious. She was obviously talking about him leaving town without a word all those years ago, for which he owed her an apology, or at least an explanation.

He cleared his throat. Ellie was still looking off the way Tyler had left in a teenage huff. Buck was used to his son's behavior by now, but he imagined it was new to Ellie.

"I'm sorry about Tyler," he began, then paused when Ellie's wide-eyed gaze flashed to him, her eyebrow raised as if to ask him a question.

"He's been through a lot." Her voice was soft and gentle when she talked about Tyler.

"And I'm sorry I didn't handle things better," Buck continued gruffly.

"You've been through a lot, too."

Buck sighed loudly. "Will you please stop making excuses for me? I'm trying to say I'm sorry."

She looked him straight in the eye. "Apology accepted," she said simply.

Buck didn't remember Ellie being so erratic with her emotions. One second she was ripping him to shreds about his behavior; the next second she was blowing it off as nothing. Even as a teenager, she'd been extraordinarily levelheaded, a characteristic Buck especially admired in her.

At least until it had come to the building of the new highway, the Texas government's bright idea to make a shortcut, a straight link between Dallas and Houston, which had caused what had once been a small, quiet ranching town to brim over with tourists. With that stupid highway forced on them, Ellie's pragmatism had gotten the best of her, not that, in Buck's estimation, the government program had done considerably much to improve Ellie's lot in life.

Therapy Ranch, indeed.

"Look," he began tentatively. "It's good I caught you alone for a few minutes. I believe I owe you an…" Here he hesitated. The first word that sprang to his lips had been *apology,* the word Ellie had just used when he'd said he was sorry, but that wasn't what he wanted to say. "An explanation."

* * *

Ellie looked at him calmly, her arms relaxed down at her sides. "For?" she inquired lightly.

Ellie already knew what this was about. It was obvious to her that Buck was carrying the weight of the world on his shoulders, and she suspected coming back to Ferrell hadn't helped matters any. As the old saying went, it was like putting salt in a wound, though admittedly Ellie wasn't certain exactly which wounds had carried Buck from Ferrell so quickly all those years ago.

Nor did she care. She was *way* past that, she told herself again. But she did want to offer her old friend comfort, especially in his time of need.

"Go on," she encouraged, rustling up a smile for him.

"I know you must have been pretty angry with me when I left the way I did." Buck jammed his fingers into his sandy brown hair, making it stand on end.

"Buck, that was twenty years ago," she reminded him gently, her tone carefully neutral. Why did he want to dig up the past when there was so much to deal with right now, in the present?

"Still," he drawled slowly. "You must want to know what happened back then."

Ellie shrugged. "If you want to tell me, I'll listen. But, Buck, the truth is, what happened all those years ago doesn't really matter to me anymore."

Buck stepped back, looking stunned, as if she'd slapped his face, not simply spoken a few quiet words.

"What?" she asked, thoroughly confused by his unusual behavior. Wasn't Buck relieved to find she hadn't been carrying a grudge all these years?

"It didn't matter to you that I left?" He arched a questioning eyebrow at her.

Ellie frowned. "Of course it mattered. A lot of people in this town thought—*I* thought—you and I had a future together. I realize now, of course, looking back on it, that it was just a teenage romance."

"Was that all it was for you?" Buck cringed. Ellie thought he looked like he wanted to yell. Or punch his fist right through the wall of the stable.

He shook his head but didn't speak right away.

"I couldn't stay in Ferrell," he said at last.

"Because?"

"Because of the development, the highway. I knew this town was a goner. It was sure to turn into a tourist trap. And it *has*," he said, sounding pleased with his own conclusions. "I noticed it the moment I returned. The town has changed, if not the people. Even my own mother sold out. She would never have turned our ranch into a craft store if it wasn't for the new tourist trade."

"So what, Buck? The neighbors are thriving, and business is good. I think the highway was the best thing that ever happened to this little town."

"Exactly," Buck replied quickly in a rush of breath, forcefully planting his hat back on his head.

"Let me see if I have this straight," Ellie said, moving to the door of the nearest stall and sliding down into the fresh straw, wrapping her arms around her knees. She wasn't sure her shaky legs could hold her much longer.

Buck didn't follow suit but rather stood over her, almost as if he meant to intimidate her.

Well, if he did, it wasn't going to work. She wasn't

going to back down to a sullen Buck Redmond just because he'd finally decided to come home.

"You left because you didn't want the town to grow and change with the development," she stated, keeping her voice in a low, careful monotone.

Buck tipped his hat in response.

"Look around you, Buck. You have to see how good it's been for everyone."

He shrugged. "If that's what they want, then I'm happy for them."

"But it isn't what *you* wanted," Ellie mused aloud. "Which is why you left."

Buck nodded. "That pretty much sums it up," he agreed fervently. "At least that was part of the reason. I was really angry when my mom sold off all the stock on our ranch. I think that was what made me snap."

Ellie didn't know whether to laugh or cry. She'd imagined a million reasons why Buck had left the way he had, and 9,999 of those reasons involved her, specifically. Despite the fact that she believed she'd put those feelings in the past, where they belonged, she could not help the joyful rush of relief she felt in finding out that Buck's leaving had had nothing to do with her.

But it did leave one question.

"Why didn't you just tell me how you felt? Back then, I mean," she asked softly, her gaze dropping to her knees. Her feelings were a little hurt now, and she didn't want that.

"Because I already knew how you felt," Buck stated plainly, crouching down on his haunches before her and sweeping his hat off his head, brushing his fingers through his thick, unruly mop of sandy brown hair.

"But I didn't know how *you* felt," Ellie replied, feeling dangerously close to tears.

Why was he bringing this up again? She was happy with her life now. In *Ferrell,* where she belonged. But there was no denying the attraction she still felt for Buck Redmond, despite everything he'd done.

"And I couldn't tell you," he answered. "Ellie, you have to admit that you were as gung ho as anyone about the highway coming through."

"What, and you didn't think I'd see your side of things?" she demanded.

"No."

His brief answer sent another stab of pain through Ellie's insides. Despite what she'd said to Buck earlier about them having a simple teenage romance, Ellie had always believed it had been more than that. Something real, if not lasting. And now Buck was saying he hadn't trusted her at all.

Not with what mattered most to him.

Not with his heart.

"You know," she said after a long, painful pause, "I still wish you would have talked to me. You didn't even try to work out things between us."

Buck frowned and shook his head. "I'll admit I took the easy way out," he said slowly, his voice gruff. "I didn't want to face you and tell you I was leaving. If I had seen you, Ellie, I might not have left at all."

"Would that have been so bad?" Ellie still couldn't look him in the face.

Buck shrugged and shook his head again. "I don't know the answer to that question, Ellie. I really don't know."

"Things didn't turn out quite the way you'd planned." It was a statement, not a question.

"No. They didn't. But life never does, does it? At least I have Tyler to show for my efforts, even though I haven't been the greatest dad. And you have your tourist ranch."

Ellie was so surprised, she stood suddenly, knocking Buck off balance and onto his backside in the hay.

He didn't know, did he? About the ranch, and the role he now played in it? Somehow she'd assumed someone had told him why he was here, besides to attend his mother's funeral.

She offered him a hand up, which he willingly took, giving her the crooked grin she'd once found so adorable, and that still did funny things to her insides.

What should she say now?

Should she be the one to tell him about the ranch?

No, she decided suddenly. *Let the lawyer do the honors*. There was no reason she had to be the one to spring such news on the man. In fact, given the circumstances, she was probably the last one who should be blabbing anything to Buck.

"Tyler is a very special kid," Ellie remarked, smiling gently at Buck.

"Just don't let him hear you call him that. He thinks he was born forty years old. And I suppose my lifestyle hasn't lent him much in that arena."

Ellie didn't ask about Buck's wife, Julie. She knew the story from Mama Esther, heard it during many of the long talks they'd shared. That Julie had abruptly deserted Buck was almost more than Ellie's mind could comprehend, but that she had likewise abandoned her own two-year-old son—well, that was entirely beyond Ellie's frame of reference. She still felt angry every time she thought about it.

"You're a good father, Buck," she stated emphatically. "Anyone who sees you with the boy can tell that."

"He doesn't think so," Buck muttered. "And I'm not so sure of that myself. He's got so much anger built up inside of him. I think he might just explode some day."

"Maybe I can help with that," Ellie offered. "My ranch is called *therapeutic* for a reason."

Buck lifted an eyebrow. "It's kind of you to offer, Ellie," he said, running a hand down his face, "but we aren't going to be in town that long."

Ellie nodded, but inside, she knew otherwise. Buck didn't know it yet, but he *was* going to stay. She had to make him stay, or everything she'd worked for her whole life would go up in smoke.

The ranch. Her ministry.

Everything.

And she wasn't about to let that happen.

Chapter Three

The reception had mostly cleared out by the time Buck and Ellie returned to the ranch house. Larry Bowman, the town lawyer, was waiting for them, helping himself to what was left over from the food folks had prepared.

Larry smiled as they entered. "I waited around," he explained kindly. "If you're feeling up to it, Buck, I thought it might be best if we tackled the reading of the will now, rather than putting it off for later. I completely understand if you would rather make it another day."

Buck hung his hat on the rack by the door. "No, Larry. Today is fine. Good, actually. I need to settle things up and be on my way as soon as possible."

Buck didn't miss the surprised look Larry flashed Ellie, but she just blinked a couple of times and then shrugged before the moment was gone.

"So, did Mama leave Ellie something in the will? Is that why she's here?" Buck asked, only mildly curious and not at all begrudging whatever his mother might have left Ellie. He knew the two of them had been close.

Larry scratched the stubble on his chin. "Perhaps we'd all better sit down," he offered, rather than answering the question directly. "Everything is laid out in the will."

"You can skip the formal stuff, Larry," Buck said confidently. "I already know what the will is going to say, and I likewise know how I'm going to handle the estate. We don't need to go line by line or anything."

"I see," Larry answered, not sounding as if he *saw* anything at all. Buck arched an eyebrow. He couldn't understand what was so complicated. His mother had been a small-town woman, and she'd lived simply. She didn't have anything of value except the craft store, and Buck *knew* he didn't want to keep *that*.

Shouldn't really come as a surprise to anyone, least of all Larry or Ellie.

"Why don't we just cut to the practical stuff and let me tell you what I want to do," Buck suggested, taking a hard-backed chair and turning it around, straddling the seat and leaning his forearms against the chair's back.

Larry pulled another hard-backed chair opposite Buck and seated himself, his back ramrod straight, and set his briefcase on his lap. Larry almost appeared tense, Buck thought, which was odd for a lawyer.

Ellie evidently preferred to stand, for she leaned her hip against the table and crossed her arms, giving Larry a warm, encouraging smile, that Buck wished, for a moment, was for him instead.

Wasn't she here to support him? It looked to Buck like all the support was beaming in Larry's direction.

"So," Buck said when it appeared everyone was as settled as they were going to get, "Mama left me the ranch, er, the craft store, I mean. That's probably the main item, right? I'm sure I'll want to select some personal items to keep, and, Ellie, you feel free to do the same. I know how close you and Mama were."

Tears formed in the corners of Ellie's eyes, but she didn't brush them away. The sight of her tears was enough to cause emotion to swell in Buck's own chest, partly over the loss of his mother and partly in sympathy for what Ellie must be feeling.

"Maybe we could go to Mama's house together," he suggested, thinking it might be easier on her. He didn't want to think about the fact that by his words he had disassociated himself from the ranch that had been his childhood home. Instead, Buck forged onward with his thoughts. "That way, Ellie, you can have first dibs at all her little knickknacks and things. I'm sure Mama would be happy to see some of her keepsakes passed down to you."

Larry looked down at the folder in his hand, then adjusted his tie at the neck and cleared his throat. His face was expressionless, but a flush was rising on his cheeks. "Uh, Buck, son, I'm not sure how to tell you this, so I'm just going to come out and state it plain. There is no ranch."

"What?" Buck knew he was squawking, but Larry's statement had hit him with the force of a semitruck. "What do you mean there is no ranch? My mama lived in that place her whole married life. She might have turned the place into a tourist trap, but she wouldn't sell it off to some stranger."

Ellie's arms dropped to her sides, and her fists grasped the edge of the table. She gave an audible huff and glared at Buck. "She did sell the store—the *ranch*, Buck. Last spring. I know this is going to be hard for you to accept. She wanted to tell you about it in person, but she became ill before she could make a trip out to see you. She didn't plan it this way."

Buck buried his head in his hands. Could this *be* any worse? "I don't get it," he murmured between his palms. "Why would Mama sell her own home? Was she too frail to run the store by herself anymore?" That didn't sound like Buck's mother at all, but he was grasping at straws to come up with any reasonable explanation for Esther's actions.

"She was lonely," Ellie said sadly, but her gaze shot fierce daggers at Buck, leaving him no doubt where she placed the blame for his mother's circumstances. "That was a big old house for her to live in all by herself. She ran her business single-handedly until the day she sold out to a neighbor, but it wasn't because she was too *frail,* as you put it."

Buck frowned. Ellie just had to rub it in that he hadn't had a close relationship with his own mother. He felt guilty enough without her adding her opinion on the matter.

"It was only when she became ill," Ellie continued, "that Mama Esther needed special care."

"She couldn't be out on her own," Larry added in a businesslike monotone, that Buck thought might have carried just a hint of a judgmental quality to it.

What was it with everyone today? They couldn't just mind their own business?

"Why didn't I know about any of this?" Buck demanded, feeling repeated sharp-edged stabs of guilt with every word Ellie and Larry said.

"Again, Buck, your mother wanted to tell you in person," Ellie reiterated. "And everything happened so fast, with the illness and all. We were all completely focused on Mama Esther. Everything else had to wait."

"Someone should have called me," Buck ground out through clenched teeth. "I should have known."

"You're right," Ellie agreed softly, though still with an edge to her tone. "Someone should have called you. *I* should have called you. But it was against Mama Esther's wishes for me to do so, and I simply couldn't bring myself to deceive her in any way, not even for you."

Buck groaned. From the clipped way she spoke, barely holding back her emotions, he knew she meant *especially* not for him. "No property, then."

The money Mama had received from the sale of the assets had no doubt gone to cover her medical expenses—maybe even a Christian charity or two, knowing his mother. Buck saw his dream of owning a horse ranch floating right out the window, but he was more heartbroken by the fact that he hadn't been there for his mother when she needed him. She hadn't even told him she was ill.

And all because of his pride.

"Actually," Larry interceded, breaking into Buck's thoughts, "that isn't precisely true. You do own property, Buck, just not the ranch you grew up on."

"What?" Buck thought he might be squawking again, but he couldn't help it. He'd never been more bewildered in his life, and on top of the roiling emotions he was feeling, the mental turmoil was almost more than one man could endure.

Guilt piled on guilt for the way he had treated his mother.

For the way he had treated Ellie.

"Your mother used the money from the sale of your childhood home to invest in another property—a working ranch," Larry explained.

A *working* ranch?

Buck straightened a little at that news. He was the owner of a working ranch?

Except that it didn't make any sense. Keeping Buck's childhood home a *working* ranch had been the subject of his argument with his mother twenty years ago. If Mama had yielded, wouldn't it have been for her own son?

Although after the way he'd acted, he guessed he wouldn't blame his mother for writing him off. Still. The pieces didn't fit together to make any kind of clear picture. "My mother wasn't interested in working our ranch, and she certainly wouldn't have been capable of working a new one."

Larry nodded gravely. "That is true. Your mother never worked the new holdings herself. At the moment, the ranch is, er, being leased out to another party."

"I see," Buck said, a plan beginning to form in his mind. This wasn't so bad. Having tenants currently leasing the ranch wouldn't make his dream impossible—just a little bit more of a hassle. The end result would be no different than his original plan—sell the ranch, take the money and run.

"So there are people renting my place," Buck asked,

fighting hard to keep the excitement from showing, not wanting to look callous in front of Ellie.

"In effect," Larry answered, flashing a brief, troubled glance at Ellie, which Buck did not miss.

What were they were keeping between themselves?

Whatever it was, it was clearly deeply bothering both of them, and neither of them would make eye contact with Buck, though he switched his questioning gaze back and forth between the two of them several times. Ellie pushed herself off the table and began pacing in back of Buck's chair.

"So I'll just give the renters a realistic notice, or offer to sell to them, if they want. In any case, I can sell *that* property," said Buck. "I don't want to be unreasonable about it, but I have things I need to do elsewhere. How quickly do you think you can wrap this up, Larry?"

"Well, there's the matter of contacting Ferrell's real estate firm, if you want to sell," Larry hedged, his gaze noticeably shifting away from Buck's.

"What do you mean, *if* I want to sell?" Buck demanded, leaning forward on his arms until the back of the chair bit into his skin. "I just told you that's exactly what I want to do. Do you have a problem with that?"

"Yes. Er, no. There are…" Larry hesitated, once again glancing in Ellie's direction. "Extenuating circumstances that may affect your decision to sell."

Buck could not imagine an *extenuating circumstance* that would make him change his mind on this, but he shrugged and nodded for Larry to continue.

Larry blew out a breath and rushed on, his words

falling on top of each other in his haste to spit the sentence out. "What you need to understand, Buck, is that you are currently sitting on the property in question. Quite literally."

It took Buck a moment to absorb Larry's meaning, but then his eyes widened and he whistled his surprise, just before his racing heart took a nosedive into his stomach. "Mama bought *this* ranch? *Ellie's* ranch?"

Ellie cleared her throat and went back to leaning on the table, where she'd been earlier. She brushed a nervous hand over her long black hair, and her gaze darted randomly around the room. She looked everywhere but straight at Buck and took her time before speaking. "Technically, Buck, it's *your* ranch."

Buck needed a minute to ingest all the information that had just been thrown at him. Mama had sold his childhood home to buy Ellie's ranch.

But why?

Nothing made sense anymore.

And where had his mother lived after the sale of their family home? Buck decided that was the first and most important question to be answered, so he stammered out an inquiry. "Wh-where did Mama live, then?"

"Why, with me, of course," Ellie answered immediately, her smile wavering as her gaze got distant and her eyes luminescent with moisture.

"Ellie was the one who cared for your mother during her last days," Larry added gently.

Buck rubbed a hand against his jaw, which was starting to prickle with a day's growth of beard. "I don't know what to say." He shook his head. "I—I guess thank you would be in order," he said, nodding his head in Ellie's direction. "I really had no idea. None at all."

"Of course you didn't," Ellie snapped and then took a deep breath in an apparent attempt to calm herself, though, from the flush on her face, Buck didn't think it was working. "No one expected you to, Buck," Ellie continued. "As we already indicated, Mama Esther wanted it to be this way. I'm sure she had her reasons."

Buck's mind was racing. Ellie rented this ranch—this *Christian therapy ranch,* which Buck had personally thought was just a fancy term for a tourist trap—from his mother. And Mama had lived with Ellie. Ellie, not Buck, had been the one to care for his mother during her illness.

Here.

Right where he was sitting.

He looked around, narrowing his gaze as he realized—now that he was paying attention to such things—that he *did* recognize some of the furniture and knickknacks as his mother's. He blew out a breath. He really must have had his head in the clouds, shadowed by grief, to have missed such an obvious conclusion. His guilt and shame at the loss of his mother were obscuring his judgment much more than he had realized.

Ellie watched the mix of emotions crossing Buck's face as he took in all this new information—hurt, anger, grief and confusion warring for prominence. She said a silent prayer for the man she'd once loved with her whole heart.

"You don't have to make any decisions today," Larry informed Buck. Larry stood and gave Buck's shoulder a conciliatory pat. "Take as much time as you need."

Buck flashed Ellie an apprehensive look, his pupils dilated and foggy, lending a grayish tenor to his eyes. He nodded slowly.

"I guess I do need a little time," he murmured, his voice ragged.

Despite the feelings warring inside her, Ellie wanted to move to Buck's side, to hug him. Just to hold him again, let him know he had a friend. But she wasn't sure how he'd take it, so she didn't move from where she leaned against the tabletop. She clasped her hands tightly to the table edge to keep from launching herself at him.

"I'm going to get out of here and give you two a bit of privacy," Larry continued, his voice as low and compassionate as always. "I'm sure you have a lot to discuss. Let me know when you've reached a definitive decision regarding the ranch, Buck, and we'll go from there."

Ellie slipped into the chair vacated by Larry, thinking it would be better to be seated directly across from Buck. She wasn't sure Buck was ready to talk about anything, but as Larry had indicated, she and Buck had a lot to say to each other—providing Buck was willing to listen to the whole story and did not just write her off without an explanation.

Ellie felt badly about not informing Buck of his mother's decisions earlier. In hindsight, she decided it had been wrong not to contact Buck immediately when his mother had become ill. But so much had happened so fast. Ellie hadn't had the time to think things through.

And Mama Esther *had* asked her to remain silent, wanting to tell Buck herself in her own time.

But as it had turned out, Esther hadn't had that time,

and Buck had been hit over the head with what must feel to him like a good-size boulder.

"I'm sorry, Buck," she apologized sympathetically, realizing she'd already said that but not knowing how else to start the conversation.

Buck buried his head in his hands with a groan and refused to look at her.

"Do you have a headache?" she asked softly, her fingers twitching with the need to reach for him. "I have some aspirin in the medicine cabinet I could get for you."

Buck groaned again, louder this time. "No, thank you. I feel like my head is going to explode, but I don't think aspirin is going to help."

He looked up at her and almost smiled, the corner of his lip twitching upward just the slightest bit. It gave Ellie hope, even that hint of a smile. She smiled broadly in return, hoping he could grasp the compassion she felt for him.

"I don't think anything will help me right now," he said with a shake of his head, which then made him wince as if in agony—which he probably was, emotionally, at any rate, Ellie thought.

"Do you want to talk about it?"

"Do I have a choice?" he grumbled.

So much for hope.

Ellie's heart dipped into her stomach, which tightened painfully. "We don't have to talk right now," she assured him, keeping her tone soft despite a rising sense of alarm, which was pealing like bells in her head. "Like Larry said, you can take as much time as you need. I'm sure you have a lot to work out in your own mind before you can even remotely consider a decision."

Buck stared at her, his emerald green eyes wide, but said nothing.

Ellie clasped her hands in front of her. "Or maybe you've already made your decision."

"Ellie," Buck said slowly, "you know that what Larry told me changes everything."

Ellie lifted an eyebrow. "Oh? In what way?"

She'd half expected him to toss her out on her ear and take the ranch over right away. He had the legal right to do just that. There were no formal rental agreements on the ranch. It wasn't that kind of relationship.

Mama Esther had very much been a mother to her, especially these past few years.

"Ellie, I'm not going to take your home away from you," Buck said as if he'd read her mind. "At least not right away, I won't."

"You must have had plans," she responded. "For the money, I mean."

"Plans," Buck repeated. "Yeah. Right. Plans." He paused and shifted, leaning heavily on the back of the chair. "I really don't know what to do now."

"It's entirely your decision, Buck," Ellie assured him, even if inwardly she felt like begging him to spare her ministry. "This is your ranch now.

"I know you said you would consider selling to me, but I'm in no position to buy."

"To be honest, now that I've had time to think about it, I'm not positive I want to sell," he said frankly. "I can't see myself moving back to Ferrell, but the divorce wiped out my savings. It's something to think on."

All the more reason Ellie could and would not ask

for favors, which left Ellie with nothing except the possibility of Buck coming back into her life on a permanent basis. She didn't know how to feel about that.

Not without him making some serious concessions to her, and she wouldn't ask him for that.

She stared out the west window, where the sun was setting, and suddenly had an idea she thought might help both of them. Maybe, just maybe, she could save her ministry after all. It was worth a shot, anyway.

"Do you and Tyler have a place to stay while you're in town?" she asked.

Buck shook his head. "Nope. Planned to stay at the ranch." He laughed, but it was a bitter sound. "Guess I should be looking for a hotel, huh?"

"Absolutely not," she said emphatically. "You two are most welcome to stay here at McBride's. It is, after all, your property, Buck."

"I don't want to impose," he said gruffly, turning his gaze away from her.

"Don't be silly. There are plenty of guest rooms here. I often have clients stay over for the week."

Buck scoffed. "Like an overglorified bed-and-breakfast?" he guessed.

Ellie bristled and clasped her hands tighter. "Not at all like a bed-and-breakfast. Actually, that's part of the reason I'm asking you to stay."

"And what would that be?"

"So I can show you what I do here. I thought maybe if you saw firsthand all the good work I'm doing here, you might…." She stopped herself from completing the sentence.

"What am I going to see, Ellie?" Buck demanded,

his voice now sounding irritated, if not downright angry. "That you sold out like the rest of the town? That you're pulling in tourists who want to see what the country life is like for a day?"

"You have no idea what I do here," she snapped back, more offended than she could say.

"So tell me," he said, not sounding as if he was going to listen to her at all.

Not really.

"What makes you think this ranch is a tourist trap?" she demanded, suddenly defensive.

"The whole town is a tourist trap now, isn't it?" he replied bitterly.

"That really bothers you, doesn't it?"

"Yep."

"Enough for you to leave town twenty years ago and never look back."

"Enough for me to leave," he agreed, his voice not giving away a hint of emotion, other than perhaps irritation. "Even my own mother sold out." He sighed. "Now tell me about this ranch. I've seen horses, chickens, goats, pigs, and I think I even saw a couple llamas out there in the field."

"Alpacas," she corrected.

"What I didn't see was cattle, or a herd of horses. So what kind of a working ranch would that make this? It doesn't make any sense."

"It will if you listen to me."

"I'll listen," he replied testily. "I'm not going anywhere until I figure this out."

Buck had always been impatient, Ellie remembered, wanting to fix the problem rather than think about it.

Ellie had complemented him, balanced his practical logic with her naturally emotional responses.

But that was then. And this wasn't going to be a quick-fix problem.

"It's a therapeutic ranch, Buck," she said, thinking that should explain a lot.

"Hmm. So it says on your sign."

"You don't know what I'm talking about, do you?"

"Not a clue," he admitted, the side of his lip curling up again. It half looked like a grimace, but Ellie knew Buck was trying, in his own way.

"I work with children who have had some kind of trauma in their young lives, and some who are physically or mentally disabled in some way. Many times the families board here, as well."

"And you do what exactly with the children?" He arched an eyebrow, daring her without words to explain her work in a way that wouldn't make him laugh.

"Introduce them to the animals. Animals are wonderful therapy, Buck. Didn't you see what Sophie did with your own son?"

Buck scoffed. "That will last all of a half hour. Then he'll be back to his old surly self."

"Perhaps," Ellie agreed. "But over time, kids bond with the animals. The goats and pigs and such help calm the children. Some learn to ride the horses. It helps them open up emotionally, connecting with the animals."

"Sounds like tourist hogwash to me."

That wasn't the answer Ellie was hoping for. She folded her arms in an instinctively defensive posture and glared at him. "It's a ministry, thank you very much. At least give it a chance," she said testily.

To her surprise, Buck nodded. "Maybe," he said in a soft, gruff voice. "I do believe I owe you the opportunity to show me what you do here—keeping in mind that I don't believe a word you're saying, of course."

Ellie shrugged and smoothed down the edges of her black knit dress. "That could change."

Buck barked out a short, crisp laugh that didn't sound the least bit cheerful. Ellie thought he might be making fun of her, with the twisted grin he gave her.

"I doubt that very much," he stated wryly. "But I can hardly kick you off the ranch without giving you a fighting chance, not after you helped my mother the way you did."

"Your mother sincerely believed in this ministry," Ellie said fervently.

"She must have," Buck agreed. "She sold her own house and bought this ranch."

"For the *ministry* we have here," Ellie repeated, thoroughly exasperated by the stubborn man.

"Ministry? Is that what you call it?"

Ellie huffed. Hadn't he seen how happy Tyler had been this afternoon, caring for the horse? The boy had a real gift, and Buck was too blinded by his own grief to see it.

Well, maybe she'd just have to *make* him see it.

"I'll make you a deal," she stated bluntly, folding her arms in front of her. "If you can take the time off work. You and Tyler stick around here for a couple of months and see how the ranch operates. You'll be back before Tyler starts school in the fall."

Buck lifted an eyebrow, but after a moment he nodded.

"I gave my notice at the Flying Pony before I came

here. It's time for me to make a change. I just don't know what, yet."

Her breath caught in her throat. Could it be that her plan would really work?

"Then you and Tyler can be my guests while you decide the course of your future. If you don't see the purpose in my ministry, I'll leave willingly, without a fight. I know you have every right to make me leave now, but I'm asking you for this opportunity to prove myself, the ranch and the ministry I do here. What do you say?"

Buck sighed and shrugged. "What can I say? It appears Tyler and I are going to be your guests for a while."

Chapter Four

Despite the nip of spring, the weather the next morning was mild enough for Ellie to wear only a light jacket out. She'd fed the ever-hungry preteen Tyler bacon, eggs and toast for breakfast, but there was no sign of Buck. When she asked Tyler about Buck's absence, he indicated, still chewing on a piece of toast loaded with strawberry jam, that his father made it a habit to get up and about early.

Not surprisingly, Ellie found Buck in the stable, still dressed head to toe in black, from his cowboy hat to his boots. He even wore a black duster. He was walking from stall to stall and making notes in a small spiral pad of paper—apparently, Ellie gauged, assessing the worth of her horses. She wondered if his desire to own and operate a horse ranch had changed—it had been his major life goal when they'd been dating so many years ago.

Ellie thought he must feel the same way about horses now as he had back then. Something like that was in a man's blood; it wasn't likely a dream he'd given up on, even if he'd pushed it deep inside his heart. She took in a deep breath of the comforting smells of horse and hay, her livelihood and her life.

"You're planning to sell the ranch in order to buy your own," she guessed aloud as she approached him from behind.

Buck jumped, obviously startled, and turned toward her, an adorably guilty frown making his eyebrows scrunch together underneath the brim of his hat.

"Uh, yeah." He sounded as guilty as he looked.

Ellie wondered whether he was tallying how much he'd make on the sale of her horses, but he hadn't yet read the will himself, and there was one small detail in the fine print that he might not be so happy to discover. Ellie guessed he'd pitch a fit when he found out the truth.

The ranch was his mother's, so it stood to reason she would have purchased the horses, as well, Ellie imagined. But in truth, the stock—all the horses and barnyard animals—belonged to Ellie. She had been making payments to Mama Esther on the land with an unspoken lease-to-own agreement that didn't involve a down payment she would never be able to afford, but the livestock belonged to her alone.

She was debating whether or not to enlighten him of this fact when he spoke again.

"It's true that I planned to sell my mother's ranch," he continued in a terse voice, sweeping his cowboy hat off his head and tucking it under one arm. "Of course, it didn't help that she'd converted the main ranch house into a craft shop, but even without that, the location right off the new highway wouldn't have been a good thing for my horses."

"How many horses do you own?"

He scoffed. "Two. Mine and Tyler's. I left them in the care of the Flying Pony until we get settled."

"Oh." Ellie paused, surprised by this new information. She would have thought Buck would have acquired a large, strong herd by now. "I thought you left town in order to buy up a head of stock and run your own horse ranch."

"That was the plan," he said, irony—and maybe a touch of regret—lacing his voice. "Life doesn't always work out the way you want it to, though, does it?"

Ellie looked him straight in the eye. "No," she said clearly. "It doesn't."

Buck had the good grace to cringe at her statement, lifting his hat and jamming his fingers through his thick, sand-colored hair before turning away from her gaze.

When he didn't immediately speak, Ellie moved back to the subject at hand—the rest of her life. Specifically, the status of her ministry, which appeared to be hanging by a precarious thread at the moment.

"You would seriously consider keeping this ranch as your own?" Ellie asked.

Buck scrubbed a hand through his hair, which was now completely disheveled; it would have given him the look of a young boy were it not for the lines on his face, lines that showed the many years of misery he'd endured.

"I'm thinking on it," he said at last, still not looking her in the eye.

"Oh," was all Ellie could think of to say.

Buck shook his head and brushed his thumb softly against the side of her cheek. His green eyes glowed emerald when he looked down at her, forcing their gazes to meet. "Don't worry, Ellie. I'm not going to renege on our deal."

"I didn't think you were."

"You'll have your two months. That'll give you enough time to find someplace else to live."

"And something else to do?"

"What?" Buck looked confused.

"My ministry?" she reminded him coldly.

"Oh, that," he said with a shrug. "Don't worry about it, Ellie. I'm sure there are tons of things you can find to do around Ferrell that would constitute a Christian ministry."

"Maybe," she agreed with an edge to her voice she could not control. "But this ranch is *my* ministry. It's unique, and it can't be done without land."

Buck shrugged again. "I can't help you with that. I have my son and myself to worry about now."

Ellie bit her lip to keep from reminding him how selfish he sounded, although caring for Tyler was a valid point. Still, in her mind she saw a great big gray area in which she and Buck might be able to come to a mutual understanding that would benefit both of them.

Buck saw only in black and white.

"I've been looking over your breeding stock," Buck said in an obvious attempt to change the subject. "I'm very impressed by your quarter horses. You picked out some very nice lines. I didn't know you were such a connoisseur of horses."

Ellie glared at him as if he were a flaming idiot. "I'm not. But your mother was."

"My mother?" Buck was clearly astounded, and it showed in the high pitch of his voice.

"You think she lived on a horse ranch for the whole of her married life and never learned anything?"

Buck shook his head. He'd never thought of his mother that way. She'd always been…well, his mother. She'd taken care of him and his father—cheerfully cooked, cleaned and washed the laundry. A loving housewife.

Now he realized he hadn't given her enough credit. He'd had no idea just how involved his mother really had been in the actual day-to-day running of the ranch.

In his own defense, he thought wryly, it was hard for any boy to see his mom as a human being, wasn't it?

That insight might well apply to fathers and sons, as well, he realized, scratching the scruff on his chin. It was definitely worth thinking on.

"My mother picked out your stock," Buck clarified, arching his eyebrow at Ellie. He couldn't help but sound thoroughly bemused. He *felt* that way.

"Didn't I just say that?"

It was like Ellie had suddenly burst Buck's bubble with a sharp needle as she continued to glare at him. He'd been lost in thought, but he suddenly realized, if her expression was anything to go by, that she was angry with him—really angry. And he supposed she had good reason, what with him hovering over her, eventually planning to kick her off the property and all. Sneaking out to take a peek at her stock when she wasn't looking.

But it was the only solution he could think of that made any sense. The way he saw it, he had two choices—sell the property, or keep it and start his horse ranch here, though the idea of staying in Ferrell didn't especially work for him. Ellie would understand how he felt and would even agree with him if she just thought it through—at least he hoped she would.

What else was he to do?

"I hope your *own* horses are equally as well-bred," she said, crossing her arms and taking a step backward.

"Why is that?"

"Because," she stated markedly, "if...*when* I leave, I'm taking every last piece of livestock with me."

He chuckled. "You can have the llamas—alpacas—whatever. And the goats. I never cared for the beasts, myself. But the horses stay here."

"My eye," she replied sharply, glaring razor-sharp daggers at him. "The land might not belong to me, but the horses do. And if I go, they go."

Buck thought she clamped her mouth shut to keep from adding a "So there!" to the end of her statement.

Whether or not she said the words aloud, her statement included them.

So there!

Her threat had infinitely more backing than she realized. To his own surprise, Buck was actually seriously contemplating keeping this land. It was located on the outskirts of town and somewhat away from the highway. But if he kept the land, there would be no money for the breeding stock he'd need to start his herd.

There was the rub.

Ellie must have been following his train of thought,

because she grinned severely up at him, her violet eyes narrowed on him.

"I see you get my point," she prodded. "Which leaves you in quite the quandary, doesn't it?"

Buck scowled. "I'll figure it out."

"I'm sure you will."

The last thing he needed right now was a sarcastic comeback. Buck jammed his hat on his head and turned to walk away without another word.

"I've got guests—clients—coming in an hour," she informed his back. "You can tag along and watch if you want."

It appeared she was holding out an olive branch to him, but he was too angry and frustrated to take it.

"I'll just stay out of your way," he grumbled without missing a step.

"Suit yourself." Ellie spun on her heels and started to leave the stable through the opposite door.

"Where's Tyler?" he queried. "I don't want him getting in the way of your *therapy* session."

Sarcastic? Two could play that game.

Ellie shot a glance over her shoulder. "In with the new foal, of course. Where else would he be?"

With that, she strode from the stable and up the hill toward the ranch house, her thick, straight, black satin hair swinging behind her. Buck watched her go, remorse filling his chest. Why did every stupid thought in his brain have to come out his mouth when Ellie was around?

It never happened with other people. In fact, those who knew him probably considered him silent and broody—which, of course, he was most of the time.

Except with Ellie.

For some unexplainable reason, Ellie always brought out the worst in him, made him speak every single thought, every feeling, right to her.

Or at her.

Of course, Ellie brought out the best in him, as well, but that was beside the point. Buck scowled again for no one's benefit but his own.

Now, he realized, his troubles were substantially multiplied, for if Tyler was in the stable with the foal, as Ellie had indicated, he must have heard the entire interchange between Buck and Ellie. Buck was having enough trouble with Tyler without adding this whole "sweep the ranch out from under Ellie's feet" thing.

With a loud sigh, he approached the one stall he hadn't yet attended to, the one he'd saved for last because he knew the newborn foal, which he thought might be exceptionally well-bred stock, would be waiting for him. Buck was anxious to see how the little guy was faring after the difficult breech birth the day before.

Buck was no longer quite as interested in the stilt-legged colt, since he had a no doubt surly son he would have to face down. Funny just how quickly a man's perspective could change.

As Buck expected, Tyler was in the stall with the newborn foal, sitting on the fresh hay, his back against the far wall, with one knee up and the other leg stretched out before him.

The boy immediately glared at him when Buck entered the stall, but Buck ignored his glowering son and instead crouched beside the colt, who was now teetering around on faltering legs. Buck empathized with the newborn—Buck himself felt like he was teetering around and faltering with every step.

His son's words confirmed his thoughts.

"You're gonna kick Ellie out of here, aren't you?" Tyler leveled the accusation at Buck with a glare that only a son could give to his father. Buck wanted to cringe.

Instead, he set his shoulders. How could he explain what he didn't know himself? His feelings for Ellie were so complex, they were like an intricate web—one that had been balled up and stuffed into his chest. No chance of sorting out that mess.

"It's…complicated," he said after an extended pause, during which he stared absently at the colt.

"You always say that when you don't want to tell me the truth," Tyler indicted, continuing to glower.

"I'm not kicking her out, exactly," Buck said, his mind racing to find an explanation that would satisfy the fuming young man. "At least not without reasonable time to find other accommodations. I think I'm being fair. Don't you remember? I promised her two months."

"Sure you did."

"Son, we need a place to live ourselves," Buck reasoned, trying his best to keep his voice level. He hated how he had to stretch to justify himself before Tyler.

"So does she."

It was no use arguing anymore, and Buck knew it. Both of them would go round and round in circles and end up where they had started.

They always did.

Buck growled and shook his head. "It's complicated," he said again, knowing that explained nothing but hoping to end this pointless conversation before it got completely out of hand. He hated arguing with his son. Tyler should know Buck's philosophy of life by now better than anyone else in the world, without him having to constantly repeat it.

What was, was.

And if that meant, in his son's words, kicking Ellie off her—*his*—land, then so be it. No sense beating himself up about it, or taking any flack from Tyler. He was giving Ellie far more notice than he would have given anyone else. Buck couldn't help it that this turn of events affected Ellie personally.

"Son, it's out of my control."

"I knew it." Tyler stood in one swift movement and stalked past his father, brushing so close he almost bumped Buck's shoulder as he passed. "You won't even give her a chance."

Buck gazed after his retreating son's back, as confounded by Tyler's behavior as he'd ever been. Buck and Tyler had never gotten along particularly well, but something had changed. Something was different now.

Ellie.

What had the woman done to Tyler that the young man was already so firmly in her corner?

Whatever it was, Buck didn't like it.

Not one bit.

Ellie tried her best to put the distraction of Buck's presence—and her looming destiny—behind her as she prepared for the day's clientele, a special favorite of hers. Children from the foster-care program for Grange County, located in the nearby town of Silverdale, were bused in every Wednesday.

To these special kids, some abandoned by their parents or truly orphaned from some type of tragedy, her services were free. So what if she wasn't making a huge profit on the ranch? she argued to herself, as if to Buck. She was helping others in need, making a real difference here.

If only Buck could see it.

Ranging in age from toddlers to teenagers, the children delighted in the ranch life they found here at McBride's. The little ones liked to pet the bunnies and chase the chickens. The older children often visited the horses. Ellie taught them how to care for the various animals and even took them on trail rides from time to time. She had purchased a pair of draft horses for special-occasion hayrack rides, which the children loved so much.

Ellie straightened her shoulders, forced a smile on her face and waved to the children as the bus approached the ranch house. She wouldn't think about the fact that the ranch would soon not carry her name, that everything she'd worked for all her life was about to go up in smoke.

She *wouldn't* think about it.

As the children clambered over each other to get off the bus, Tyler appeared at Ellie's side. She was surprised but tried her hardest not to show it, giving Tyler the same smile she offered the children running in her direction.

"Are these some of the kids you minister to?" Tyler asked, curiosity lining his expression.

"They are," she replied, giving the boy another big grin. "All of them come from one bad situation or another. I'm sure you can imagine how difficult it is for them to lose their families and then have to trust a new group of people with their well-being. Foster homes aren't always as permanent as they need to be. Not too many of these children ever get adopted. Not enough, anyway."

Tyler frowned. "That's too bad."

He sounded sincere. Eager, even. Ellie wondered why Buck had indicated he had such trouble with the boy. Tyler had been nothing but sweet to her.

Tyler jammed his hands into the front pockets of his blue jeans. "Is there anything I can do to help, Miss McBride?"

Ellie couldn't believe how well mannered Tyler was acting. A little shy, even. This time her smile was as much inward as it was outward.

"Why, yes," she replied readily. "I can use all the help I can get around here."

"What would you like me to do?"

Ellie thought for a moment before speaking. "There are a couple of things that come to mind," she said slowly, waving at the foster-care children as they ran past her and into the farmyard. "I'll tell you what. How about if I tell you what needs doing and you pick what you'd most like to do yourself?"

Tyler nodded solemnly, his lips in a serious straight line. "Sounds good to me."

Ellie gestured toward a flock of warbling preschoolers. "Those little guys need someone to watch over them. They always send a supervisor from the county, but as you can see, she's really got her hands full. You'd just need to watch them, keep them out of trouble. Mostly they like to pet the smaller animals and chase the chickens around the pen."

Tyler laughed.

"Or," Ellie said with a wink, "you could go back down to the stable, where most of the teenagers hang out. I think there are a couple of pretty girls."

Tyler's face blushed as red as a Macintosh apple, and Ellie had to smother her chuckle. For all her blustering to Buck, she didn't know all that much about twelve-year-old boys. Tyler probably wasn't into girls at his age, she thought. Maybe she shouldn't have teased him that way.

Tyler glanced toward the stable. Despite her joking, Ellie fully expected him to pick the latter of the two options, to be with kids his own age—not to mention being in the atmosphere in which he was most at home. With horses.

But the young man surprised her. He shrugged and said, "I'll watch the little ones, I guess."

Ellie's eyebrows rose in surprise, but she beamed at Tyler, nonetheless. "Excellent. The woman in charge over there is Mrs. Downey. Just tell her you're there to help, and she'll point you in the right direction."

Tyler looked at his feet, where he was swishing around the dirt with the toe of his tan cowboy boot. "Thank you," he muttered, so low Ellie could barely hear him.

Ellie didn't think her smile could get any wider, but it did. "No, Tyler. Thank *you*."

Buck didn't leave the stable after his confrontation with Tyler. He was most at home among horses, and their sounds and smells somehow comforted him.

He sighed aloud. When had his life gotten so outrageously complicated?

When Ellie McBride had walked back into his life. That was when.

He heard rather than saw the group of loudly chatting teenagers enter the stable, and he quickly moved to the far corner and into the shadows, where he couldn't be seen.

Where had these kids come from, and what were they doing in Ellie's—in *his* stable?

To Buck's surprise, the rowdy group immediately quieted upon entering the stable. Even more astonishing, they all picked up grooming tools, and each went to work on a different one of the horses. Obviously they'd been here before, and each teenager appeared to have chosen a horse they particularly liked.

One of the girls squealed in delight upon finding the newborn colt in the birthing stall, and all the teenagers crowded around, straining to see the foal. There were delighted whispers all around as they observed the mother horse with her baby.

"Look at him. He's trying to walk," said one of the teenagers.

"How cute. His mother is nudging him with her nose, trying to encourage him," said another.

"Maybe we ought to back off." This came from one of the older boys. "I'm not sure she wants us all bothering her and her foal right now."

The kids murmured in agreement and wandered back to the horses they'd started to groom earlier.

Buck hadn't been noticed yet, and he had no intention of being seen now. He quietly strode to the back entrance of the stable and slipped out the partially open door.

He wasn't sure what he'd just witnessed, but he made a mental note to ask Ellie about it.

Why would she possibly let a group of teenagers onto her land, much less trust them with her horses? Was this what she was getting paid to do?

And how, Buck mused, was this any sort of ministry? Free stable help, maybe, but nothing Buck himself would consider using with his own horses.

Buck began to trek up the hill, toward the ranch house, his black boots sliding on the coarse gravel. He immediately saw that the property was overrun with small children dashing this way and that. Attempting to avoid little children was the last thing Buck wanted to deal with right now, but there was no other way to get to the house, so he moved forward again, determined to walk right through the middle of the chaos.

And then he saw Tyler.

The boy was sitting on the ground, cross-legged, with a little boy—maybe three or four years old—on his lap. He was holding a squirming white rabbit in his left hand and gently guiding the child's touch with the other. Both his son and the little boy were chuckling at the rabbit's antics.

The Texas landscape in this part of the country was dry and pretty sparse, especially in early spring, after the tough winter, but the ranch house had a few blooming white flowering dogwood trees tucked around it, and Buck quickly stepped behind one, hiding himself from view as he gazed at his laughing son.

Buck tried to remember the last time he had seen Tyler laugh, really laugh, as the boy was doing now. To his regret Buck couldn't think of a single time in the past couple of years. Buck's life had been on a downward spiral for the past few years since the divorce, and he now realized with a deep stab of remorse that he'd taken his son right along with him for the ride.

Tyler was surprisingly gentle with the little boy, though Buck knew his son was inexperienced with preschoolers. Tyler was typically a loner, shying away even from kids his own age back at the ranch Buck used to run.

"Pet the bunny," he heard Tyler instruct the squirming child in a tender but eager tone of voice. "See how soft his fur is? Nice bunny."

The little boy on Tyler's lap giggled as the bunny sprang loose from his hand and scampered off under the safety of one of the nearby rabbit hutches.

Buck had to clamp his lips together to keep from laughing out loud himself. It was such a rush of relief to see true joy on his son's face.

What kind of a father had he been to Tyler, anyway? No wonder the boy was so sullen. Why hadn't he tried harder to give his son a better life? Had he been so wrapped up in his own problems that he hadn't really noticed his son as he should?

Buck knew that was true. Yet here at Ellie's ranch, and apparently under Ellie's guidance, the boy was opening up like a flower to the sun.

Amazing.

Making a good deal of noise by shuffling his feet on the gravel, Buck stepped from behind the tree and walked casually toward Tyler, pretending he hadn't seen the interchange between the young man and the preschooler at all. Still, he grinned and winked at Tyler as he passed, and to his surprise, the boy smiled back.

As Buck neared the ranch house, he glanced over his shoulder to find Tyler now leading a small group of pre-schoolers into the large wired coop for a chicken chase.

"Get one. Hurry. There's one over there," Tyler urged, followed by his own laughter and that of the children. "Oh, I almost got that one."

Naturally the children would never catch the chickens, and Buck suspected Tyler wouldn't, either, though the boy clearly could if he wanted to. It was the playful interaction with the little ones that Tyler was obviously seeking, although becoming a caretaker to preschoolers was the last thing on the planet Buck would ever have pegged his son for.

He shook his head at the thought, then removed his hat and hung it on a hook as he entered the house. He hadn't seen Ellie around the property and figured she was probably inside somewhere, and he was deter-mined to find her. After what he'd just witnessed, he had far more questions than answers.

Chapter Five

Buck found Ellie in the kitchen, preparing tuna-fish sandwich wedges for the children. She looked up as he entered, but didn't smile or even acknowledge his presence. Buck grunted softly and pulled a chair out from the kitchen table, turning it around so he could straddle it.

When Ellie glanced at him again, it was with one dark eyebrow arched and her head cocked a little to the side. "Do you ever seat yourself normally at the table?" she asked wryly. "Like a regular human being?"

Buck looked down at his arms, which were resting on the chair's back, and chuckled. "Honestly, I never thought about it. Tyler and I normally ate in the bunkhouse with the other cowboys, and all we have at *our* dinner tables are benches."

"That explains it, then."

Buck suspected the *it* in question was Ellie's idea of good manners, and he had the niggling urge to stand up and turn the chair around to suit her.

That wasn't going to happen. He shifted more solidly into place on his *backward*-facing chair.

Ellie sighed deeply. "What do you want, Buck? I'm kind of busy right now."

"Anything I can do to help?" he asked before thinking better of it.

"You know your way around the kitchen?" Her lips quirked in amusement.

"No."

"Then, no, there's not anything you can do to help. Thank you, anyway."

"Can we talk about the ranch, then?"

Ellie stopped slicing sandwiches and closed her eyes, taking a deep breath to steady herself. *Please, Lord,* she prayed internally, *give me grace to get through this.*

When she opened her eyes, she squared her shoulders and took another calm, cleansing breath. She knew what Buck was asking, what with the ranch currently overridden with children of various ages. What she didn't know was how he would respond to what she would tell him.

She *needed* to make him see that what she was doing was important, a real ministry and not simply running an overglorified tourist trap, as he had so un-aptly put it. Ellie just wasn't quite sure how she was going to do that.

No words immediately came to mind, no matter how hard she prayed and searched for them. Buck's gaze was as reserved as always, and he never took his piercing green eyes off her for a moment.

She thought about playing innocent, making Buck say what was on his mind, but quickly discarded that idea in favor of forthrightness, knowing Buck was more apt to respond to a straightforward question than to her beating around the bush.

"What is it you want to know?" she asked with all the dignity she could muster.

"Well, for starters, why are there a gazillion kids running around the ranch?"

Ellie shrugged. "It's part of my therapy program. They are the kids from the foster-care program in Silverdale. They get bused in every Wednesday afternoon."

"I see," Buck said, though he clearly didn't. "And they are here to do what, exactly?"

"Interact with the animals, mostly. Animals can be great therapy, you know, especially for a child who has trouble bonding with human beings."

"Chasing chickens is good therapy?" There was a bit of a teasing tone to his voice, but Ellie knew Buck was ultimately serious about the question, just as he was dead set on removing her from this property.

"Sometimes," she answered slowly. "Mostly that's just for play. But you ought to see the children with Cody, my German shepherd. When the dog encounters a distressed child, he'll nose his way under the boy or girl's arm, in effect giving them a furry hug."

Buck nodded for her to continue.

"Most of the teenagers like the stables the best. They work with the horses—grooming them, fixing tack, cleaning stalls. Oddly enough, or rather by God's grace…."

She paused when Buck cringed visibly and looked away from her. "By God's grace," she repeated, "each teenager in this particular group has bonded with a different horse. They are always anxious to get out to see 'their' horses, without ever arguing about who gets what mount."

"Yeah, I saw that," Buck commented with a gruff edge to his voice.

"Did you?"

"I was still in the stable when they came in."

"Did they see the foal?" Ellie asked, not realizing until after she'd spoken the words that she might well just have unintentionally changed the subject, which was the last thing she wanted to do. She desperately needed to clear up Buck's misconceptions about her ministry.

He chuckled. "I'd say they were pretty excited about that particular find."

Ellie smiled. "Good. I'm glad."

"I watched them for a few minutes. They all seemed to know their way around horses. How is that?"

She shrugged. "I taught them."

Buck gave a low whistle. "That must have taken a good deal of time and effort."

"Maybe," she conceded, cutting the sandwiches into quarters so they were easier for the small children to eat. "But it was worth every second. And I happen to enjoy working with kids."

Buck laughed. "That much I got."

He was suddenly silent and his smile faded. Ellie was curious and a little frightened by Buck's suddenly quiet demeanor, but she waited for him to speak.

"I saw Tyler on my way up to the house." He spoke casually, but Ellie knew there was a lot more emotion behind those words than Buck was letting on. "He was helping a little boy with one of your rabbits."

"That was nice of him." She kept her hands busy, hoping Buck wouldn't see that she was shaking with determination, and maybe a little bit from dread.

"Hmm," Buck answered, now sounding thoroughly bemused. "Yeah. Nice of him."

It wasn't like Buck to repeat words. He was definitely the strong and silent type. Ellie knew there was something that had rattled him enough to shake him from his stupor.

Seeing her ministry for what it was, maybe? Did she dare to hope?

"See, here's the thing," Buck continued. "My son doesn't like little kids."

Ellie cocked an eyebrow. "You're sure about that? Because when I was out there before, he appeared to be enjoying himself as much as the preschoolers."

Buck nodded. "Doesn't that beat all? Back at the ranch where we've been living, Tyler pretty much kept to himself."

"Just like his father," Ellie muttered under her breath, but apparently it was loud enough for Buck to hear, because his gaze narrowed on her.

"I—I didn't mean anything by that," Ellie stammered hastily. The last thing she wanted to do right now was rile Buck up. Next thing she'd know, she'd be packing her bags, no explanation wanted or given.

"No. You're right," Buck agreed with a clipped nod and a soft chuckle. "My son *is* like me. That's why I can't figure out what's going on now."

"Maybe Tyler is just learning to relax," Ellie suggested tenderly. The soft spot in her heart was for Tyler, of course. At least that was what she told herself.

"You know, you could do with a little R & R yourself, Mr. Ranch Foreman."

"Hmm," he said again, as if the thought had never occurred to him before.

"Your room and board are on me," she reminded him. "Well, not exactly. But the rent I'm paying covers the mortgage on the ranch each month."

Which was sort of true. At least it had been until Mama Esther had passed.

Ellie realized Buck hadn't heard the entire will, though probably he had guessed the truth. With Esther's passing, Buck now owned the ranch free and clear. All the more reason for him to give Ellie her notice—so he would finally own some land of his own with no strings attached.

His own horse ranch.

The one dream, Ellie suspected, he'd never quite released, even when everything else in his life had gone sour.

Ellie knew she should share the information, but she remained silent. He'd learn about it soon enough. She needed as much time as she could get between now and then to prove what she had here was a bona fide ministry to the children and that he should keep her on past the end of their two-month agreement.

Buck lifted an eyebrow and blew out his breath. "If you don't mind my asking, how much does the government pay you for this weekly therapy?"

Ellie hoped Buck didn't notice her change in demeanor, because that was the one question she *didn't* want him to ask. Hastily, she picked up the platter of tuna wedges. "I need to get these out to the children."

Buck stood and was blocking her path out the door faster than she thought possible. *Cowboy reflexes,* she thought miserably. And Buck looked like a big, black-clothed brick wall—no way to get over, under, around or through him. At least not until she'd answered his question. And it didn't help that her heart began to flutter at his close proximity.

"I'm waiting," he said, staring down at her and crossing his arms over his chest.

Ellie looked down at the tray in her hands, not able to bring herself to make eye contact with him.

"Nothing," she murmured under her breath, fighting the urge to squirm under his narrowed gaze.

"I'm sorry?" Buck said. "I don't think I quite heard that."

Oh, he'd heard it all right. Ellie was sure of it. He was just making her repeat it to torture her. She looked up at him, locking gazes with him testily.

"Nothing," she repeated irately, much louder than she needed to speak.

"Nothing," Buck parroted. "Ellie, you aren't going to tell me you're giving your services, whatever they may be, away for free, are you?"

Ellie refused to look away, no matter how scathing Buck's gaze was on hers.

"Sometimes," she admitted. "To the kids who really need it. The government can't afford to pay. Or rather, they have too many other expenses."

Buck huffed. "I imagine they do."

Ellie glared at him. "I won't turn these children away. Not as long as they need what I offer."

"But this is a business, right?" He didn't sound like he believed that it was.

"It's a ministry, Buck," she said, tired of repeating herself. "I do what I do to serve God and others. But, yes, in answer to your question, I do actually make my living on this ranch, thank you very much."

"By giving everything away for free."

"No." She wanted to shake Buck until he could see the truth—until his teeth rattled, as a matter of fact—but she doubted it would help. The man clearly had rocks in his head. "I have many clients who pay for the therapy program. The foster-care program just doesn't happen to be one of them."

"I see," Buck said, nodding to himself as if he'd suddenly stumbled across the truth. "So that's where the tourists come in—and the bed-and-breakfast you insist you don't run here. To pay for the foster-care kids. I guess that makes sense, in a cockeyed sort of way."

Ellie sighed loudly, clenching the platter in both fists, willing herself not to toss the entire sticky contents right in his face. He was baiting her deliberately, and they both knew it.

"Ellie?" he said when she didn't rush to explain herself.

"No." She shook her head fiercely. "They aren't tourists. Or at least, not many of them. Most of the kids come from Ferrell, and some from neighboring towns."

"How do you advertise?"

"Word of mouth, primarily. The *Tri-County News* occasionally writes an article about the ranch. I'm a member of a national organization. Now, if you'll excuse me, I need to deliver this snack to my little kiddos."

Buck raised an eyebrow but stepped sideways, out of the doorway. "This isn't over."

Ellie scoffed and stepped through the doorway, not looking back. "Whatever you say, Buckshot," she replied, purposefully using the same pet name she'd had for him when they were youngsters, hoping it would throw him off a bit.

It must have, because he didn't say another word, although Ellie could feel his eyes on her back all the way down the hill. She smiled to herself. She wasn't done fighting for this ministry.

Not even close.

Buck was still mulling over Ellie's use of her special pet name for him the next morning, over a hot cup of coffee. Ellie had remembered that after all these years? He remembered all too well. How could he have walked away from that kind of love?

Ellie and Tyler were nowhere to be seen. They were probably not even awake yet, he guessed. It had long been Buck's habit to watch the sun rise, and the fact that he was currently unemployed and taking a little R & R, as Ellie put it, didn't keep him from waking before dawn.

This wasn't rest *or* relaxation.

This was torture, plain and simple. He and Ellie couldn't say a single word to each other without undertones of unspoken dialogue—why she wanted to stay on at the ranch and why he couldn't let her do so.

If it were anyone else renting his ranch, Buck would have sent them packing the moment he'd learned about his mother's will. But Ellie was his tenant, which changed everything, and they both knew it.

Count on Ellie, though, to try to take advantage of his generosity to plead her case. Why couldn't she just realize she wasn't going to get her way in the end and start looking for somewhere else to do her *ministry?* It sure would make it easier on both of them if she would.

But Ellie had always been a stubborn woman. There was no reason to think she'd be anything else just because twenty years had gone by.

Not his Ellie.

No. Not *his* Ellie.

Buck knew he needed to stop thinking that way, or he was going to end up in a world of hurt. He was obviously already headed in that direction, and it wouldn't take much to send him right over the edge. He sighed deeply and took another sip of his still-steaming coffee.

He was so startled by the sharp rapping on the front door, he nearly spilled his coffee in his lap. Surely Ellie didn't have clients calling at this time of the morning?

Standing stiffly, he jammed his hands through his hair and stretched. Only two days with Ellie and he was already getting soft in the head. He promised himself a good long horseback ride—to clear his head—later on in the morning and moved to the door, pulling the curtain slightly to one side so he could peer into the early morning mist.

Travis Martinez.

And with what looked to be a dozen red roses, not so hidden behind his back, and a goofy grin on his face. It didn't take Buck more than a millisecond to figure out what *that* meant.

Buck's hackles were up faster than a cat with its tail

on fire. He didn't even stop to think why and had the itching desire to slam the door closed on wide-smiling Travis before he'd even opened it to the man.

Travis Martinez, Buck remembered, had been the male lead in the same musical where Buck had first noticed Ellie. Travis had been in the same class with Buck, but where Buck had been the football hero, Travis had been the drama geek. Their paths had rarely crossed back then.

But Travis wasn't the same gangly boy Buck remembered. He had, Buck acknowledged crossly, grown several inches since high school and had filled out a bit. And if Travis's toothy-white grin was any indication of his feelings, the man still carried a torch for Ellie, just as he had in high school, even if at the time Ellie had never had eyes for any boy but Buck.

At least back then she hadn't. He hadn't a clue what kind of man Ellie was attracted to these days. Maybe a man like Travis.

Maybe *Travis*.

Seething with pent-up frustration, Buck twisted the door handle and plastered what he hoped was a smile on his own face, though he was certain he failed in the effort.

Travis looked more than a little startled before his smile widened, were that possible. "Buck Redmond. I didn't think you were still in town."

"Well, I am," Buck replied testily, even as he stepped away from the door and gestured Travis inside. "I'm staying with Ellie, at least for the time being."

"Oh," Travis said, sounding as surprised as he looked. "I, uh, I'm glad to hear it."

Travis didn't *look* glad to hear it, Buck thought. In

fact, Travis's expression registered quite the opposite. He was obviously sensing some kind of competition with Buck, though for the life of him, Buck couldn't imagine why. What Ellie and Buck had shared had been a lifetime ago.

Still, it soothed Buck's ruffled feathers a little bit to think that he might still be considered *competition* where Ellie McBride was concerned. Even if it wasn't true.

"Why don't you come into the kitchen and have a seat, Travis?" Buck said, gesturing with a jerk of his chin to the dining table. "How do you like your coffee?"

Travis sighed and pulled the roses from behind his back. "I wasn't planning to stay, actually. I was driving by and I saw Ellie's light on, so I thought I'd stop by and give her these," he said, tossing the bouquet on the table.

"She's not awake yet."

"Oh." Travis sounded positively dejected, and for some reason that made Buck want to grin. As popular as Buck had been in high school, he'd never been a bully, but for some reason he had the most peculiar yearning to push Travis's buttons now.

"I'll let her know you were here," Buck said with a casual shrug he wasn't feeling. He flashed a peripheral glance at Travis but didn't square off his gaze. "You can leave the roses. I'll be sure Ellie gets them."

"Be sure I get what?" asked a sleepy-eyed Ellie from the back-porch door. She was casually dressed in gray sweats and a bright red T-shirt, and her shiny black hair looked adorably rumpled from sleep, Buck thought, his heart pumping furiously despite his best efforts to remain calm and aloof. He just hoped Travis didn't notice Ellie the way he did.

Travis was already on his feet, sweeping up the bouquet of red roses and thrusting them at her, another silly grin plastered on his face. Buck wanted to roll his eyes.

"I bought these for you yesterday," Travis said in a rush, "but I got hung up at the school."

Ellie smiled sweetly at Travis, making Buck want to pound on something, put his fist through a wall, maybe. Ironically, in the same moment he was thinking about how little Travis knew Ellie, unless she'd changed more than Buck knew, though this was something a woman wasn't likely to change her mind about over time, was she?

Ellie's favorite flowers had always been violets—the color of her eyes.

"I'm the drama teacher at Ferrell High," Travis explained for Buck's benefit. "And I got roped—unwillingly, mind you—into the planning committee. Which is going into overdrive, I think," he continued with a chuckle.

Buck scowled at no one in particular. "Planning committee for what?"

Travis glanced at Buck in surprise and then turned his gaze back on Ellie. "Our twentieth class reunion. Didn't you get an invitation, Buck?"

"No," Buck snapped, wondering why he cared.

He *didn't* care. He just didn't want Travis here.

"Well, Cindy Spencer is in charge of sending the invites," Travis explained. "I expect she thought you left town after your mother's funeral, and didn't know where to send your mail. I'll be sure to let her know you're still around."

"Thanks," Buck said gruffly. He scoffed inwardly, though he kept his expression carefully neutral. Like he'd go to his twenty-year class reunion. That wasn't going to happen.

Ellie hadn't yet accepted the bouquet from Travis. She was staring at Buck as if he'd grown a third eye.

"Actually," Travis continued, "that's part of the reason I'm here. The reunion, I mean."

"What about it?" Buck queried, leaning a hip against the table and crossing his arms. He knew Travis's statement hadn't been aimed at him, but he didn't really care if he was intruding.

The answer to Buck's question was patently obvious, even before Travis uttered a word of explanation. They'd already clearly established that *Buck* wasn't the reason Travis was here, reunion or no reunion. But if Travis thought for one second that Buck was going to concede and give the two of them a moment of privacy, he had another think coming.

"I, uh," Travis stammered, clearing his throat and tossing a pleading look toward Ellie, which Buck didn't miss.

"Buck," Ellie said, her tiny hands cocked on her hips, "can you *please* give us a moment?"

Buck shrugged but didn't move.

Ellie sighed loudly and shook her head, clearly exasperated with him.

"No, it's okay," Travis said in a vain attempt to relieve some of the tension in the room. He was still holding the flowers out to Ellie, apparently frozen in that position, Buck thought with a scowl. "I don't mind if Buck is here. He'll find out soon enough, anyway.

I've come to ask you to be my date to the reunion. I know you'll have your own reunion next year, but I'd be honored if you'd be my date for mine."

Ellie glanced quickly in Buck's direction. He looked like a stone statue, his jaw set and his arms crossed. He was so still, it didn't even look like he was breathing. If it wasn't for the pulse beating a steady rhythm in the corner of his clenched jaw, Ellie might have wondered if he were alive at all.

He certainly wasn't giving away what he was thinking, but Ellie could guess. The two men were looking at each other like fighting dogs across a ring. They were practically baring their teeth and growling at each other. All they needed was a little drool, and the picture would be complete.

"Buck," she pleaded, hoping beyond hope he would be reasonable, but Buck had never been reasonable, at least where Ellie was concerned. He had always been overprotective of her, though the one time she'd suggested it might be jealousy, he'd practically bit her head off. Even in high school he'd give a warning growl to any boy brave enough to approach her, so no one ever did.

At the time she hadn't minded. She had been head over heels in love with Buck Redmond and hadn't so much as noticed any of the other guys around her. Funny how twenty years could change a woman's perspective on things.

Buck wasn't the only man in Ferrell, and it was high time he figured that out. So why did a small part of her secretly wish he would suddenly do a one-eighty and sweep her into his arms and fervently declare that no man but Buck himself would take her to the reunion?

Ellie eyed Buck again, but he hadn't budged, so she turned to Travis and gave him her best smile, determination setting in over any wavering she was feeling in her heart. She snatched the bouquet of roses from his hand and inhaled deeply.

Roses were okay, though she preferred violets. "I would be happy to be your date for the reunion, Travis."

Travis's genuine grin was surprisingly hard for Ellie to bear. Why did she feel guilty?

"I—I'd better put these in water," Ellie stammered, clutching at the bouquet of roses. She spun around and left the room before she could see the expression on either one of the men's faces. She already knew Buck would be blowing steam out his ears, despite the fact that they no longer had a relationship. And poor Travis... Ellie thought she might back out if she saw whatever mix of fear and elation was crossing that man's face.

She needed to make a stand with Buck, and this date with Travis was as good a situation as any she could have dreamt up. She only hoped the poor sweet drama teacher didn't get caught in the cross fire.

Buck didn't move for a moment after Ellie left the room. His head was swimming with emotion. The pointed glance Ellie had given him before she'd answered Travis had left him dumbstruck.

What had she expected Buck to do? Ask her to be *his* date to the reunion? He hadn't even been invited to attend—not formally, anyway.

Even if he had been invited, why would Ellie think he wanted to go at all? Ellie, of all people, should know by now how much his life had changed in the twenty years since he'd graduated high school. What was left for him to come back to?

It was only then that he realized Travis was staring at him, openmouthed in expression, if not in reality. Buck scowled at him.

What was the man waiting for, anyway? He'd gotten the answer he'd come for.

"I, uh, I'm sorry if I intruded," Travis said tentatively, brushing his short, straight dark brown hair out of his eyes with the tips of his fingers.

"You didn't," Buck said tersely.

"Well, I mean, I guess I thought when I found out you were still around, that you might have wanted to take Ellie to the reunion yourself."

Buck leveled his gaze on the man, who, he thought with just a touch of amusement, looked like he was quaking in his boots, completely insecure and unsure of himself. "And why would you think that?"

"You and Ellie were quite the item in high school," Travis reminded him in a low voice.

"I remember." This time Buck couldn't stifle his laughter. "And?"

Travis grabbed the back of the nearest chair and swallowed hard. "Is it okay if I sit?"

Buck shrugged nonchalantly, and he was still grinning. He couldn't help himself. "Suit yourself."

Travis brushed his hair back with his fingers again, and Buck recognized it for what it was—a nervous habit. Travis cleared his throat several times but couldn't seem to get any words out. Buck decided to help him.

"I take it you and Ellie are dating?"

Travis's eyes widened to enormous proportions,

but as his gaze met and held Buck's, he gave an agitated chuckle. "Not exactly. I've asked her out enough times over the years, but she always turned me down. Until today."

Travis grinned, and Buck wanted to floor him.

"Over the years?" Buck asked before he realized he didn't really want to know. Besides, he was prying into Ellie's business when he had no right to do so. What had happened to the close-lipped cowboy he'd thought he'd been?

Ellie McBride. That was what had happened.

"I'd say it's been at least three years since the first time I asked her out," Travis explained hesitantly.

Buck gave a low whistle. "That's a lot of time."

Travis sighed. "Tell me about it. I've tried everything in the book, but I just can't get her to accept me as more than a friend—not that I've given up on her."

Buck nodded. "I can see that. Ellie can be pretty stubborn about some things."

"You're telling me."

"Well, partner, I wish you the best," Buck continued. In his head he added an unspoken *You're going to need it.*

Chapter Six

It was a beautiful morning, and Ellie was sitting on the back-porch swing with her Bible in her lap. For as long as she'd been living here at the ranch, her favorite time of day was the early morning, her quiet time, when she could read the Bible and pray about the day ahead of her.

She'd been trying to read a psalm, but despite her best efforts, she just couldn't concentrate. Her mind kept wandering back to the morning two days earlier, when she'd woken to find Buck and Travis facing off over the kitchen table. It was a good thing testosterone wasn't flammable, or she could have lit a match and the whole ranch would have exploded.

What was with Buck, anyway? And more to the point, why did she care?

They'd avoided talking about Travis ever since that morning. Come to think of it, Buck had avoided Ellie altogether, either making excuses to go into the town or else secreting himself in the stable.

Ellie snapped her Bible shut with a loud sigh. For a moment, when she first walked into the room that morning when Travis was there, she'd thought Buck was acting a bit territorial toward her—and the worst part was, she'd *liked* it.

Even with Travis in the room. Ellie felt a pang of guilt even now, for she knew she shouldn't feel anything for Buck, not after all this time. Travis was her, well, her, uh, friend. Or at least that was what she kept telling herself.

Travis hadn't made any secret of his feelings for her, and Ellie couldn't say she was completely surprised that he'd shown up at her door and asked her to the class reunion. She knew he wanted to marry, settle down and start a family. He'd told her as much on several occasions.

So far, she'd managed for the most part to avoid those conversations, though until Buck had arrived back in town, she'd never known quite why she felt that way. She just wasn't ready for that big of a commitment, she'd told herself repeatedly, though in truth she wasn't sure she completely believed her own propaganda.

But for all that, Travis wasn't her greatest concern at the moment. Buck was here now, and she had to deal with him—more precisely, with her latent feelings for him, which she hadn't even realized she possessed until that moment. The fact was, when Travis first asked her to the reunion, she'd hesitated *because she'd hoped Buck would ask her.*

And what kind of stupidity was that?

She stood in a huff and shook her head, though there was no one around to see it. So much for her quiet time.

"Get over it," she muttered crossly to herself as she went back into the ranch house.

If only it were that easy.

Ellie's morning client arrived at that moment, knocking at the front door. Buck and Tyler were seated in the dining room, eating cold cereal for breakfast, but Ellie dashed across the room before they could rise.

"I'll get it!" she exclaimed, a good deal more cheerfully than she felt.

Her heart rose the moment she opened the door to little Morgan and her smiling mother. Seven-year-old Morgan was a new client, with the sparkling eyes and joyful smile of a Down syndrome child. Her mother, Marty, a single parent and a new resident of Ferrell, looked hopeful.

"I see you're wearing your cowboy boots," Ellie observed, speaking directly to Morgan with a gentle smile.

Morgan returned the grin with natural exuberance. "Going to ride a horsey today."

Ellie nodded. "That's right. Are you ready to be a real cowgirl, Morgan?"

Morgan's mother laughed. "That's all she's been talking about all week. Horsey this, horsey that."

"Then let's get started," Ellie suggested, throwing a glance back toward the table where Buck and Tyler were seated. "Tyler, would you mind saddling Pal for me?"

Pal, an aptly named palomino quarter horse with a large white blaze on his muzzle and four white socks, was the gentlest gelding in her stable and the horse she always used with physically impaired youngsters.

"Sure thing, Ellie," Tyler replied enthusiastically.

Ellie smiled back at him. The rough, surly boy she'd first encountered was long since gone, at least with her. In his place was a happy young man who loved to help out around the ranch, especially with the animals. Ellie had quickly noticed his natural kinship with the animals and let him spend as much time with them as possible.

Good therapy for the boy, she thought with a sense of contentment and a bit of pride.

But, of course, she wouldn't tell Buck that, not that he would listen to her if she did.

"I'll help," Buck growled under his breath, obviously not really wanting to help at all.

Ellie wondered why he'd offered. Probably to get away from her.

Ellie and Morgan arrived at the corral just as Tyler was leading Pal from the stable. Ellie had carried a safety helmet out with her and now placed it on Morgan's head, fitting the strap securely under her chin.

Morgan made a groaning sound from her chest and started pulling at the helmet. "Bad hat," she said several times as she tried to dislodge the helmet with her hands.

Morgan's mother made calm, soothing noises. "You have to have a helmet to ride the horsey," she explained calmly.

Morgan shook her head and glared at her mother and then at Ellie.

"Bad hat," she said again.

"Look, your horse is here," Ellie said, trying to distract the little girl from the worrisome helmet.

"Horsey!" Morgan exclaimed, running straight for Pal. The palomino nickered but didn't shy away. Ellie had carefully trained him not to spook at quick movements.

Morgan slid to a sudden stop, raising up a cloud of dust by her feet. She turned and rushed back into her mother's arms before Ellie could say a word.

"What's wrong?" Ellie asked gently.

"No horsey," Morgan said, her voice muffled from her mother's sleeve.

"But, honey, you've been waiting all week to ride the horse," her mother said serenely, coaxing Morgan inch by inch back toward the animal.

"No horsey," Morgan said again.

"Okay," Ellie said immediately. "No horsey, Morgan. You don't have to ride today."

A disabled child balking at the horse was another problem she often encountered, and once again she knew just what to do about it. With most children, whether physically or mentally impaired—or both, as with little Morgan with her Down syndrome—it simply took a little bit of persuasion and a lot of patience to work through the heart of the problem.

There was no reason Morgan had to ride today. It often took several weeks before a child was acclimated to the large animals. Patience in Ellie's job was definitely a virtue.

Morgan smiled shyly when she realized she was getting her way.

"You don't have to ride the horse," Ellie repeated in her most reassuring tone. "But how about we just go up and pet him? Pal is a very nice horsey, and he especially loves to be petted by little girls like you."

Morgan didn't look convinced, but she allowed her mother and Ellie to lead her to Pal. Tyler was still holding the bridle loosely in his grip.

"You want me to tie him off, Ellie?" Tyler asked, giving Morgan an understanding smile.

"You know, I think it would be better if you would stay here and help me out," Ellie said, shooting the boy a smile. "That is, if you don't mind."

Tyler nodded, his grin widening, this time directed at Ellie. "Yes, ma'am. I mean, no, ma'am. I don't mind at all!"

Ellie brushed one hand across the horse's withers and the other down the soft blaze on his face, soothing the horse at the same time she showed Morgan what to do. "See? Pal likes it when you pet him. Now it's your turn."

Ellie backed up slightly as Morgan stepped in front of her. Ellie kept Morgan close enough for the little girl to feel Ellie's presence behind her as she hesitantly touched the horse's chest. When Pal swung his head over to investigate his new friend, Morgan gave a high-pitched scream and scrambled backward, right into Ellie's waiting arms.

"It's okay," Ellie said, smiling at Morgan. "Pal just wants to see you and get to know you better. He won't hurt you. See?" Ellie rubbed her hand up and down Pal's muzzle and scratched the area between his nostrils. "Tyler, would you be a dear and hold Pal's head securely for me?" Ellie asked, keeping her gaze on Morgan. "That might make it easier for Morgan to pet him."

"Sure thing," the boy replied, his face reddening from Ellie's casual endearment. Murmuring softly to Pal, Tyler reached forward to grip the bridle under the horse's chin. "I've got the horsey now, Morgan, nice and tight. Don't be afraid. Pal won't move his head anymore," Tyler said in the high-pitched tone grown men usually reserved for children. It made Ellie smile.

"Does…does he bite?" Morgan asked in the slow drawl typical of a Down child.

"Pal never bites," Ellie assured her.

"And I've got a good hold on him," Tyler added in a soft, reassuring voice. Ellie wondered if it was emotion causing the young man's voice to crack a little when he spoke, or if it was just his age.

Either way, Ellie's heart leapt, especially when Morgan smiled shyly at Tyler and didn't back away to hide behind her mother, as she tended to do with new people. Tyler was as much a natural with children as he was with animals, and Ellie said a quick, silent prayer, thanking God for bringing the boy into her life.

Even if it was only temporarily, until Buck kicked her off the ranch.

Even if getting the chance to know Tyler meant having to deal with his impossibly frustrating father.

It took a good minute for Morgan to make up her mind, but eventually she stepped forward and, with Ellie's help and encouragement, gave Pal a soft pat on the withers. When Tyler carefully allowed the horse to bow his head, Morgan reached up on her own accord to feel Pal's soft, silky mane.

"Good horsey," Morgan said, now smiling. "He's really soft. Especially his hair," she added, indicating the horse's long, flowing mane.

Tyler flashed Ellie a bright-eyed, sparkling glance of shared amusement between the two of them. Horses were covered with hair, of course, but sweet, innocent little Morgan saw only Pal's mane—and maybe his tail—as hair.

"Do you want to get on the horsey?" Morgan's mother asked, gesturing to the saddle.

Morgan shook her head vigorously.

"Don't worry, Mrs. Miller," Ellie said, rubbing a hand across Morgan's shoulder. "We are in no rush here. Often it takes time for the children to get used to the animals. We can take it as slow as you want. Morgan doesn't have to ride today."

"Oh, yes, she does," said Buck from behind her.

Ellie whirled to find Buck smiling down at the little girl, his cowboy hat in his hands. As usual he was dressed head to toe in black. He nodded courteously to Morgan's mother. "My name is Buck Redmond. I, uh, help out around here. Is it all right with you if I give it a whirl?"

Ellie's jaw dropped as Buck took the therapy session right out of her hands in a single second. She would have argued with him if it weren't for her clients being there. What right did he have to butt his nose into her business?

Literally her *business*.

The big lug.

Marty Miller, clearly taken with Buck's easy manner and no doubt his rugged good looks, nodded vigorously for him to continue with Morgan.

Buck grinned and winked at Ellie. He wanted to laugh at the expression on her face—half astonishment and half anger. She sure hadn't expected him to come forward and offer to help. As it happened, he'd surprised himself by the effort.

Now that he was here, however, Buck couldn't help but tease Ellie a little bit. He knew she must be seething inside that he'd come and busted into her *therapy* session without so much as tipping his hat in her direction.

Buck wasn't even sure why he'd come forward at all. He had been watching the whole episode from the shadow of the stable door, completely unnoticed by both Ellie and her clientele. Which was just how he liked it.

He'd been surprised when Tyler stayed around after saddling the horse, as he'd been asked, but then, his son had been spending a lot of time at Ellie's side this past week.

And it was *not* jealousy flaring in Buck's chest.

He turned his mind back to Ellie, the beautiful woman he couldn't break his gaze from. Buck was amazed at the way Ellie worked with the little girl. She was so patient and kind, and he could tell from the sparkle in her eyes that her heart was in it.

No doubt a part of that *faith* she was always talking about, as well, though Buck still scoffed at that notion as much as the idea of a therapy ranch itself. But there was no doubt to even the most casual observer that the woman had a real gift with special needs children of all types; Buck had to give her that.

Except in this case, Buck thought he could do one better, and he wasn't going to stop until he'd given it his best shot. It wasn't an attempt to outdo Ellie, of course. He wouldn't stoop to anything as petty as that.

It was just that up until today Buck had been nothing more than an observer in Ellie's world. He'd watched her with an amazing array of children, from toddlers to teenagers and everything in between. Ellie knew how to make them laugh and play—and forget about their problems for a while.

Even more surprising was the change that had come over Tyler. Buck's own son was carrying his weight around the ranch, doing chores and helping out with the kids whenever he was asked—and sometimes, Buck thought, even when Ellie didn't outright ask Tyler for help.

How could Buck do any less?

He hunkered down beside the small girl, knowing his size might intimidate her and wanting to be on the same level with her when he spoke.

"How's my little cowgirl?" he asked, keeping his voice low and even.

"Horsey!" Morgan replied excitedly.

"That's right. Horsey. And I'll bet a true cowgirl like you wants to ride the horsey, don't you?"

"Buck, if she doesn't want to—" Ellie began, but Buck cut her off with a wave of his hand.

Morgan stared anxiously at the nickering animal. Buck could easily see it from her point of view. Pal must seem gigantic to the child, and that was when the horse was standing still—never mind when he shifted around and made noise.

Buck remembered the first time he'd ever ridden— the fear he'd felt but not wanted his father to see. He hadn't backed down from riding despite the claws of fear clinging to his chest, but he remembered how much he'd wanted to. Riding a horse for the first time was scary to a kid—any kid.

What he had to do, he realized, was show Morgan how easy it was, and that she didn't need to be afraid of being up in the saddle on Pal's back.

But how was he supposed to do that?

His own father had just tossed him into the saddle and told him to hang on. Buck didn't know that much about Down syndrome children, but he was certain his own father's gruff tactic wasn't going to work for Morgan, and it sure wouldn't go over well with Ellie and Marty, which for some reason seemed nearly equally important in Buck's mind.

He thought for a moment before settling on a plan. Rather than force the already frightened child onto a horse she wasn't ready for, Buck would show the child how it was done. Maybe then she wouldn't be so afraid.

"All right, cowgirl," he told Morgan with a smile and a wink. "I'll tell you what. I am going to hop up on Pal and ride first so you can see what a good horsey he is. After that you can give it a try—if you want," he said, tacking on the ending for the ladies' benefit. Buck had every intention of seeing Morgan ride today, even if Ellie and Marty didn't know it yet.

"Morgan already said she doesn't want to ride today," Ellie informed Buck in a tight voice. "Don't force her."

Buck leveled Ellie with a gaze just short of a glare. "Nobody's forcing anyone to do anything," he said slowly and distinctly, imitating Ellie's wry tone. "All I'm going to do is show her how a cowboy rides a horse, okay?"

Ellie glowered at him and crossed her arms. "Be my guest, Mr. Know-It-All."

Buck chuckled under his breath, definitely not loud enough for Ellie to hear. She was in enough of a huff already without him getting into more trouble.

Ellie was so beautiful when she was angry that it made Buck's heart turn over. How in the world had he ever walked away from this woman, left the town, and Ellie, behind? He shook his head, unable to answer his own question.

Attempting with little success to put Ellie out of his mind, he jammed his fingers through his thick, unruly hair and planted his cowboy hat on his head. Now wasn't the time to be distracted by thoughts of Ellie.

Approaching the horse, Buck mounted easily and then turned his attention to his son, who was still holding Pal's head. "I need you to lead Pal around the corral a few times. Slowly, at a walk. Just take it easy, son."

Tyler nodded, but Buck couldn't help but notice the smile had gone from his son's face. What had he done to make Tyler suddenly turn back into the sullen boy he'd known for years?

He hadn't said anything wrong, he was sure of that. Yet it seemed to Buck that his just being in the same room—the same general vicinity—riled Tyler up, especially next to Ellie's calming influence.

Buck didn't like it, but he sure didn't know what to do about it, either. Maybe Tyler just responded to Ellie because she was a pretty woman. Who knew what ran through that boy's head?

As Buck allowed Tyler to lead the horse around the ring, he focused his thoughts on what might make the little girl feel a little safer around the animal. Buck knew he could ride Pal bareback, blindfolded and with his hands tied behind his back, but Morgan saw only a man on a horse.

He needed to show her what *she* should be doing, not show off his own prowess in the saddle.

It went against every principle he knew as a cowboy, but he slid his hands from his thighs to the saddle horn, holding it lightly but with what he hoped looked, to Morgan, at least, like a firm grip. He knew he wasn't fooling Ellie, who was as much an expert rider as he was himself.

Buck glanced down at Ellie as he passed by Morgan and the women and was surprised to see her looking up at him with what he thought might be admiration in her eyes. Gone was the glower, replaced by at least a *hint* of a smile.

So he'd done something right this time, had he?

Maybe Ellie was right. Maybe there was such a thing as a miracle, after all. The thought made him chuckle, and Ellie raised an eyebrow as if to ask him what he thought was so funny. Buck tried to wipe the grin from his face but knew he failed.

After a few turns around the corral, Buck decided his idea had worked. Little Morgan was practically glowing and was dancing around, again eager to be near the horsey.

"Hey, Tyler," Buck called down, "stop in front of the ladies, now, will you?"

Tyler glanced up at Buck, and Buck was surprised to see the boy was smiling. Well, not smiling, exactly, but there was definitely a smirk on his lips. Probably from seeing the ridiculous way Buck was riding the horse, gripping the saddle horn and all.

Buck supposed he should be offended that his son was secretly laughing at him, but for some reason, he couldn't muster up any real emotion. At least not *that* kind of feeling. He grinned back at Tyler, belatedly identifying his true emotion.

Pride.

Tyler, Buck suddenly realized, was growing into a man Buck could be proud of.

Was proud of.

He wished he knew how to tell Tyler that, but Buck knew he'd never come up with the words, so he just smiled back at his son and hoped that was enough.

Tyler pulled the horse up as instructed, sliding his fist up the reins to regain his firm hold of Pal's head.

"Okay, little lady, are you ready for a ride?" Buck asked Morgan, who was once again pulling against the straps of her safety riding helmet and only half paying attention as Buck dismounted Pal and crouched before her.

"Is that strap too tight under Morgan's chin?" he asked, directing his question to both women simultaneously even as he reached to check the helmet for himself.

"No," Marty answered directly. "Morgan doesn't like anything covering her head. It's just one of those things we have to deal with. She's especially sensitive around her face. I'm not letting her ride without a safety helmet, though."

"Of course not," Buck and Ellie said at the same time and then glanced at each other in surprise. Once upon a time they had often done just that—said the same thing at the same time. Finished each other's sentences.

Buck cringed inwardly. *Back in the day.* It took Buck by surprise that so many things between him and Ellie were still the same even after all those years apart, and his heart lurched uncomfortably in his chest.

"Bad hat," Morgan said with a petulant frown, which Buck found endearing.

"Come on over here, cowgirl," Buck instructed, inspiration hitting him like a lightning bolt. "Let's go take another look at the horsey."

Hand in hand with Buck, Morgan approached the side of the horse, looking up at Buck as often as she did the horse.

Ellie held back a grin, but she was smiling inside. When Buck and Tyler had first started sharing the ranch with her, she had been surprised to discover that Tyler, whom she'd first classified as shy, was so good with children. Now she was seeing firsthand where the gift came from.

Strong and silent—like father, like son. And Buck's gift with children… Well, that was obvious, too. God had had His hand in this even before Ellie had recognized it.

She wondered if Buck realized the magnitude of this moment, of what he was accomplishing out here today. Not only was he pitching in, but he was actually working out Morgan's therapy—better, Ellie acknowledged to herself, though she would never admit as much to Buck, than she could have done.

"It's important for you to wear a helmet," Buck said, his voice low and soft. He swiped a glance at

Ellie. "You have a man-size helmet around here some-place?" he asked in a whisper.

Ellie's gaze widened and she was certain her jaw dropped.

Buck Redmond in a helmet? A man who'd been riding horses practically since before he was walking?

Cowboys didn't wear helmets, though most English riders did.

But as fast as those thoughts flashed through her mind, Ellie saw where Buck was going with it, and a new sense of appreciation and gratitude washed over her so strongly, it brought tears to the corners of her eyes, which, naturally, she fought to hold back. It wouldn't do to have Buck see how much his thought-fulness affected her.

Ellie dashed to the stable and came back with an adult-size helmet in one hand. Buck swept his cowboy hat off his head and dangled it from the saddle horn as he put the helmet on his head and adjusted the straps under his chin with a no-nonsense movement that surprised Ellie.

"See, Morgan, you're just the same as Cowboy Buck," Marty told the little girl, excitement and bewilderment fighting for prominence in her tone.

Cowboy Buck.

Now Ellie really wanted to laugh.

She pinched her lips together, but when she looked up at Buck, he was staring straight at her. She tried her best to keep a straight face but just couldn't do it, and in the end a chuckle escaped despite her best efforts to keep it inside.

Buck scowled, but she could see from the twinkle

in his eyes he didn't really mean it. Despite his gruff exterior, he was laughing with her.

"There's one more thing," Buck said, lifting his cowboy hat by the crown. "A real cowgirl needs a hat."

With that, he placed his own black Stetson on Morgan's head. Because of the helmet Morgan already wore, the cowboy hat actually fit rather well, Ellie thought, and it certainly made the little girl grin from ear to ear.

"Is it okay if Tyler lifts you up here in front of me?" Buck asked Morgan as he swung into the saddle. "That way we can ride the horsey together, and I can hold on to you real tight so you don't fall off."

"Yes, please, Cowboy Buck," Morgan said with the pure delight of a child.

As Tyler wrapped his hands around Morgan's waist and effortlessly lifted her into the saddle, in front of Buck, Ellie's chest swelled up with so many emotions, she couldn't even begin to sort them out. And when Buck spoke directly to Morgan, encouraging her to relax and have fun with the horsey, Ellie flat out wanted to kiss him.

Well, maybe not *kiss* him. That was pushing the envelope further than she wanted to even think about.

But even in the short time she'd known the Miller family from the local church, Ellie had seen how many people talked *about* Morgan and not to her, as if she weren't standing right there. Many people were afraid of children with disabilities like Morgan's, and that fear caused them to talk over her or ignore her completely, averting their eyes from her as if it was polite not to look at all. Or as if what Morgan had was contagious.

But not Buck. Since the moment he'd shown up on the scene, he had looked the child straight in the face with a smile that didn't falter a bit. If he was uncomfortable with Morgan, he sure wasn't showing it.

Neither was Tyler, for that matter. Ellie's heart nearly burst. She was proud of both her men.

Whoa. Not *her* men.

Ellie was slipping fast, and she knew it. She mentally scrambled to higher ground as Tyler slid the reins over the horse's neck and Buck took control, urging Pal into a slow walk.

Morgan gripped the saddle horn with both hands and squealed with delight, but Buck had firm control over Pal and the horse didn't so much as sidestep. "Look there, Morgan. You're riding Pal. You're a real cowgirl now," he said, his voice ripe with enthusiasm and encouragement.

"Nice horsey," Morgan replied.

Buck laughed. "Yes. Nice horsey."

"Buck is wonderful with Morgan," Marty commented to Ellie as they watched him walk the horse around the corral with seemingly endless patience at the little girl's excited outbursts and never-ending questions.

"Isn't he, though?" Ellie responded thoughtfully. No one could have been more surprised by this turn of events than she was. She was seeing Buck through new eyes, with perhaps a pinch of nostalgia mixed in with it.

She'd thought everything had changed since Buck had left town. Now she wasn't so sure. Maybe the old Buck *wasn't* gone forever, as she'd previously supposed. Maybe he was tucked down somewhere behind that rugged cowboy exterior.

Time and tragic life events had certainly left their marks on Buck; there was no doubt about that. But now Ellie wondered just how much things had really changed.

Seeing Buck's smile as he rode around with Morgan pretty much clinched it for Ellie.

She was in deep water, and she wasn't sure she knew how to swim.

Chapter Seven

Buck stalked toward his closed bedroom door, then did a swift about-face, his black cowboy boots sliding effort-lessly on the plush maroon carpet, and stalked in the other direction, toward the window, where the darkening shadows signaled dusk over the Texas plain. He jammed his fingers through his thick hair, spiking it in every which direction, and then shoved his hands into the front pockets of his black jeans as he reached the window, turned abruptly and strode back toward the door.

He was wearing a proverbial trail in the carpet. At this rate he really was going to end up forging a path in the thick shag that Ellie would never be able to vacuum out.

He felt like a caged tiger, but he wasn't about to leave this room—his self-imposed *cage*. Buck knew himself well enough not to subject himself to a ready-made torture device, even if he wasn't all that much more comfortable staying in his room.

Travis was on the other side of that door, all dressed up for the reunion and waiting for his date.

Ellie.

Buck didn't know why it bothered him so much. He had no claim on Ellie. Travis had been pursuing a relationship with Ellie for years, if what Travis had told him was true. Buck was relatively certain the man hadn't just been spouting nonsense in order to keep him away from Ellie.

Certainly Travis felt competitive when it came to Ellie, not that Buck could blame him. Buck felt a little bit territorial himself, even if he had no right to be.

As if Buck were competition.

He scoffed audibly. He wasn't any kind of threat to Travis. If Ellie thought of Buck at all, he was sure it was only as an opponent—a dictator, even. Some awful entity about to drive her from her own home.

Which he was.

Only, it was starting to bother him.

He should have forced his hand right from the beginning, given Ellie two weeks' notice and taken the ranch for himself. Instead, he was Ellie's guest in what felt like *Ellie's* ranch, and was even participating in what Ellie termed her *therapy*.

And he *liked* it.

It made him feel good, and Buck couldn't remember the last time he'd felt truly happy. In helping Morgan, he'd somehow helped himself.

Buck paused as he heard the sound of voices, Travis's eager hum and Ellie's quiet laugh. Buck swallowed hard and clenched his fists against changing his mind and stalking down the hallway and into the living room.

After what seemed like a lifetime, the front door opened and closed.

Good.

They were gone. Buck let out a breath he hadn't even realized he had been holding. With effort, he unclenched his fists. The reunion would last for several hours. Buck no longer had to stay cooped up in this room.

He stood silently for a moment, letting his emotions wash over him, hoping they would recede if he just let them go.

Anger. Frustration.

Jealousy.

Jealousy.

Who did he think he was kidding, anyway? He shook his head as if in answer to his own unspoken question. He didn't want Ellie going to the reunion with Travis. Buck didn't want her anywhere near the man.

He wanted her with *him*.

And he was acting like an immature adolescent, pacing ineffectively around his room instead of taking action. That wasn't like him.

The cage was open. The tiger was loose.

Resolutely, Buck moved to the bedside table and opened the drawer, looking for a pen and paper to write Tyler a note to let him know where he was headed. Tyler was out with some of his new friends, but Buck didn't want him to worry if for some reason he got home early and found Buck gone.

And Buck *would* be gone.

He glanced down at the drawer and chuckled despite his black mood. The drawer was meticulously organized. He found a thick pad of paper with the therapy ranch logo across the bottom, two blue pens and a Bible.

Just like a hotel, Buck thought, only the Gideons hadn't placed this Bible here.

Ellie had.

Picking up the soft leather-bound Bible and thumbing distractedly through the pages, Buck wondered if Ellie had placed the Bible there for his sake or if it was something she did in all her guest rooms.

He remembered a time when he and Ellie kept each other accountable in reading through the Bible every year. Prayed together about their future. It had been years since he'd even cracked the cover of the Holy Scriptures.

Too long.

He shook his head and placed the Bible where it had been, scooping up the pad of paper and a pen and scrawling a hasty note to his son, which he planned to leave on the kitchen table on his way out.

He glanced in the mirror and took a quick inventory of what he was wearing. A black Western shirt and black jeans. Same as he always wore.

He considered changing his clothes for about one millisecond, then shrugged and combed his fingers through his ruffled hair as he reached for his hat. His clothes were clean, and he looked like he always looked.

Good enough for the reunion.

The music, which had moments before been an uptempo country song, slowed down. Ellie felt more than saw Travis reach for her in the semidarkness of the Ferrell Rangers' home gym, lit only by stage lights and a sparkling silver glitter ball twirling slowly over their heads.

"I'm parched," she said with a quick step backward.

Travis looked disappointed, but he nodded. "I'll get us some punch. Be right back, okay?"

Ellie nodded absently, her mind distracted from Travis's words. She wasn't really that thirsty. She just didn't feel like dancing with Travis right now.

Which wasn't fair to him and she knew it. Nor was it fair the way her eyes kept wandering back to the door every time there was some movement there. People walked in and out regularly, friends she'd known her whole life.

But none of them was Buck.

And every time it wasn't him, a new stab of disappointment hit her chest. Buck had stated quite clearly he wouldn't be coming to his twenty-year reunion, but Ellie held out hope he'd change his mind, though she refused to acknowledge why that mattered to her one way or another.

"You dance with the guy that brought you," her father used to say. And that was what Ellie was doing—but for all the wrong reasons. She wondered for the millionth time if she'd made a mistake accepting Travis's invitation to the reunion.

Her own reunion was up next year. Maybe she should have waited until then—and attended without a date at all.

Travis returned to Ellie's side with two cups of frothy punch. He handed her one, and she sipped absently, not really tasting the tart beverage. She just wanted to call it a night and go home, but the reunion had barely started. She wouldn't do that to Travis. He was too good of a friend. It wasn't his fault Buck Redmond had suddenly returned to town.

She smiled up at him, though her heart wasn't in it. Travis deserved better than she was giving him, and she rallied herself to try to be a good date. When the music sped up to a lively Texas two-step, Travis set Ellie's cup down on a nearby table and gestured to the dance floor.

"I, uh, never really learned to do this dance," she said, stalling awkwardly. *So much for being a good date,* she thought, although the part about her not knowing how to do the dance was the honest truth.

"That's okay. I'm not a great dancer, either. We'll just have to wing it. Nobody's watching us, anyway." Travis held out his hand to her.

Ellie shrugged and, against her better judgment, allowed Travis to lead her out toward the middle of the gym. He spun her under his arm as they walked.

"This is nice, isn't it?" he asked a little too brightly. Ellie could feel his discomfort and knew she was the cause. She wondered if he could feel her tension, or see it even, written plainly in the expression on her face.

She had to try harder. Maybe everyone wasn't watching them, but what if her anxiety was obvious to even the casual onlooker, to her friends and neighbors? She didn't want to be the topic of gossip any more than she had to be, and she knew Buck being in town and living at her—*his*—ranch, was already more fodder for the old mill than she would have liked.

"It's lovely," she answered, smiling back at him. That wasn't a lie, anyway. The planning committee had outdone themselves with the blue-and-silver decor and Ranger memorabilia. "Don't blame me if I step on your toes, though."

"No problem," he replied with a chuckle. "I just hope I don't step on yours."

Travis had no sooner grabbed her hand and put his arm around her shoulders than she felt the jarring motion of another man's hand slapping Travis's back.

"Hey, buddy, you don't mind if I cut in, do you?"

Buck.

Dressed head to toe in black, he looked as handsome as she'd ever seen him.

Didn't the man have another color in his wardrobe? she thought irritably, trying to keep her mind off the way her spirit had picked up with Buck's arrival.

Ellie might not know how to do the two-step, but her heart obviously did, as it thrummed wildly in her chest. She swallowed hard and glanced at Travis, whose expression was likewise registering shock, though she knew his reasons were completely opposite of her own staggering emotions. Travis looked more than a little put out by Buck's sudden presence, never mind his brash request, but his polite smile quickly returned.

"Certainly," Travis said in a voice that didn't contain even a hint of disappointment, at least that Ellie could tell. He even grinned at her as he spoke to Buck. "She's all yours."

Travis was a genuinely nice man, but Ellie wondered how difficult the words were for him, and she felt a stab of guilt for deserting him this way, not that Buck would have taken no for an answer, as both she and Travis well knew.

Buck looked like he'd just roped a steer at a rodeo, and anger surged past her surprise. Who did he think he was, showing up so unexpectedly and then unrepentantly butting in on her dance with Travis?

Never mind that she'd been keenly watching the door for the past hour. Never mind that she hadn't really wanted to dance with Travis in the first place, since she had two left feet.

"I don't know the two-step," she ground out through clenched teeth. She brushed Buck's hand away when he made to put his arm around her.

Buck just threw back his head and laughed before grabbing her hand and dragging her back to the dead center of the floor, where everyone in the room would see them together. "That's okay, sugar. I've learned a few things since we were kids, and one of them is how to dance the Texas two-step."

"Peachy," Ellie mumbled under her breath. The overbearing oaf wasn't going to take no for an answer, and she didn't want to create a scene, so she followed him, pulling back as much as possible without being obvious about it.

Buck didn't seem to notice, or else he was ignoring the blatant signals she was sending him.

He swung to face her, pulled her tight and grinned down at her. "Just hold on, sugar, and enjoy the ride."

That was the second time Buck had used his old endearment for her. Didn't he realize how much it hurt her every time he acted like the years hadn't separated them?

Ellie had no more time to think, for Buck was a man of his word. She was swinging back and forth so wildly, her head was whirling, and not just from Buck's sudden appearance at the reunion. Buck was spinning her around with cheerful abandon, but he obviously knew what he was doing.

And he was absolutely correct about her not having to know the steps. Under his expert tutelage he simply swung her exactly where she needed to be, and his gentle hands guided her so she didn't even have to think about her feet.

After a few minutes she was even starting to have fun, hooting and hollering along with Buck and the rest of the crowd swinging around the floor to the cheerful beat of the music. Buck had always been athletic, but she didn't remember him being such a good dancer back in high school.

Of course, they'd only danced the slow songs at Buck's junior and senior proms. Ellie hadn't attended her own senior prom, since Buck had up and left Ferrell without a word. Several boys had asked her to be their date, but she had politely declined. It wouldn't have been the same without Buck.

Buck sensed Ellie's reticence as he pulled her closer into his arms when the music once again slowed. He wanted to ask her what was bothering her, but he suspected he already knew.

His presence.

The memories.

The callous way he had cut in on Travis. He really was the insensitive brute Ellie no doubt thought he was. He tucked his chin into her shoulder and inhaled, savoring the crisp country scent that was Ellie McBride, like a cool breeze through a meadow full of Texas wildflowers. She smelled the same as she had at his junior prom, their first real date together. And she looked every bit as good in her ranger-blue cocktail dress tonight as she had in the gown she'd worn twenty-one years ago.

He hadn't been able to resist her then, and he couldn't resist her now.

Why else would he be here?

He knew perfectly well he was going to set the town gossip up to breaking a new record, which he had no inclination to do. He was also keenly aware that he'd probably upset Travis, and he'd have to apologize for that later. But he could no more avoid this moment than stop himself from breathing.

It was time to stop running.

"Do you always wear black?" Ellie suddenly asked him, her tone clearly annoyed.

Buck leaned *away* from her so he could see the expression on her face. She was scowling, with a full-fledged frown on her lips, but he thought he detected the hint of a sparkle in the depths of her violet eyes.

"Why?" he responded, trying to keep the joy he was feeling from showing in his voice. "You don't like black?"

"Well, not *all* the time," she responded crisply. "I mean, I don't think I've seen you dressed in any other color since you came back to Ferrell. I know with the funeral and all…." She came to a halt. "I'm sorry, Buck. I didn't mean to bring that up."

Buck squeezed her tight. "It's okay, Ellie. I miss my mother, but I'm dealing with it."

"Yes, but you're still wearing black. This isn't the Middle Ages, you know. There's no mourning period to observe."

He chuckled. "It's nothing like that," he assured her. "I just don't own any other color of clothes."

"Seriously?" she asked, her voice rising in pitch. "You're kidding, right?"

He shrugged. "I like black."

This time it was Ellie who chuckled. "I guess."

"Now it's my turn to ask a question."

"Okay," she said, flipping her long, straight black satin hair out of her face with a toss of her head. "That sounds fair."

"I'd wait on making that assessment until you've heard my question."

"Should I be afraid?"

"Maybe," he said, but he shook his head at the same time he voiced his opinion, knowing full well he was sending her a mixed message.

Ellie laid her head against the broadness of Buck's shoulder, and once again Buck inhaled her fresh scent. "Then don't ask," she whispered.

"But I need to know," he said close to her ear.

"Okay," she whispered back. "Ask away."

"Who took you to your senior prom?"

Ellie froze in his arms, and Buck immediately wished the words back. But it was too late for that now.

"Why do you want to know?"

"Call me curious."

"Call it none of your business."

"Okay. It's none of my business. Tell me anyway. Was it Travis?"

"No, it was not Travis," she said, perhaps a little louder than she should. Several heads turned in their direction. "Don't you think if I had a relationship with

Travis back then that I'd have married him by now?"
she asked in a lower voice.

Buck shrugged. "I guess. Who was it, then?"

"No one."

"What?" Buck didn't think he'd heard her correctly.
There was no way Ellie would have found herself
dateless to her own prom. She had been and still was
a beautiful woman inside and out, and everyone had
known it—especially the guys in her class.

"I didn't go to my prom."

And it was Buck's fault.

She didn't have to say the words aloud for the fact
to linger between the two of them.

Buck didn't know what to say. He'd been so selfish.
He'd thought of Ellie every day after he left, but he'd
not often considered how much his leaving would affect
her. Somehow he'd assumed she'd bounce back, go on
with her life as if she and Buck had never been a couple.

"It's hot in here," he said suddenly. "Do you want
to go for a walk or something?"

"It *is* warm," she agreed, then broke away from
him, heading for the nearest exit without another word,
and without looking back to see if he was following.

"Hey, wait up," he called, but Ellie didn't slow her
pace. Buck had to jog to catch up with her as she quickly
paced down one of the high school's long hallways.

"Where are you going?" he asked when he caught
up to her side.

"Anywhere but here," she said, a little out of breath
from the pace she was setting. "It's so stuffy in that
gym I can hardly breathe."

Buck reached for her elbow and pulled her up short.

"You're not planning to take off because of me, are you?" he asked her directly. "Because if you are, I'll just leave now, and you can go back to your date."

Ellie stared him straight in the eye. "I'm not cutting out. I'm taking a walk to get away from the noise. As I recall, it was your idea in the first place."

"Then you don't mind if I join you?"

"Are you asking me or telling me?" she demanded.

Buck held both hands up, palms forward. "Asking. Only asking. Like I said, if you want me gone, I'm gone."

Ellie sighed loudly. "I don't want you gone."

"Good," Buck stated with a firm nod, "because I really didn't want to leave."

Ellie laughed. "But you would have. Did you find your manners somewhere when I wasn't looking?" she teased.

"As a matter of fact, I did," Buck replied at once. "In the drawer of my nightstand."

Ellie looked confused. "What?"

"The Bible," Buck reminded her softly.

"Oh." Ellie continued walking, this time at a slower, more contemplative pace.

"Are you walking anywhere in particular, or are we just rambling?" he asked, attempting to change the subject to something less uncomfortable for both of them.

"Rambling," she said, but in moments they had entered the theater auditorium, where Buck had first noticed Ellie back in high school.

"I found a lot of comfort up onstage," Ellie said wistfully. "I liked acting, becoming somebody other than who I am, even for a short while."

"I like who you are." Buck's throat had tightened to the point where he felt as if he was choking on the words.

Ellie gave him a surprised glance and kept walking until she was up onstage. Buck followed at a distance.

"Be right back," she said and disappeared backstage, behind the curtain.

In moments the stage lights were flipped on, set by set. Bright colors in a number of hues nearly blinded Buck as he stepped onto the stage. He wondered how the actors could stand it and held a hand over his brow to shade his sight.

"Ellie?"

"Here," she said from right behind him. He whirled around to see her smiling at him.

"Should you be messing with the lights?"

"I don't see why not. I worked in the backstage crew for both my freshman and sophomore years. I know how to run the light board, and I'm not hurting anything."

"Yes, I guess so." Buck walked to the edge of the stage and sat down, dangling his legs over the side and leaning back on his palms. "You had some good times here."

Ellie slipped down beside him, so close their arms were touching. "If I remember correctly," she said slowly, "*we* had some good times here. Don't you remember?"

"I remember the first time I ever saw you onstage," he said. "You took my breath away."

"As I recall, you stood outside the dressing room, waiting to introduce yourself to me."

Buck smiled whimsically. "Yeah. I'd never been so nervous in my life. I felt like I was waiting for a celebrity, and I wasn't sure you would go out with me."

"You weren't sure if a drama geek would go out with the captain of the football team? Give me a break."

Buck threw back his head and laughed. "Okay, maybe I might have been a little more self-assured than that."

"A little?"

"Hey, you went out with me, didn't you?"

Ellie nodded.

"Like I said. Good times."

"That wasn't what I was thinking of, though," Ellie said, her gaze distant under the spotlights.

"What, then?"

"You don't remember, do you?"

"That depends on what it is I'm supposed to be remembering," he said, leaning forward to stroke a stray lock of hair from her eyes. His fingers brushed her soft cheekbone, and Buck suddenly remembered a lot of things about Ellie, things he'd tried for twenty years to forget.

"Think junior prom," Ellie suggested, leaning into his touch and meeting his gaze softly.

"Junior prom," he repeated, as if he had no idea to what she might be referring. In truth he knew exactly what she was talking about. He hadn't forgotten, but he thought he would tease her a little. "What about it?"

"Oh, I give up," she said, leaning away from him with an audible huff of breath. "If you can't remember, I'm not going to tell you."

Buck laughed aloud, the sound echoing through the empty theater. He leaned forward, reaching to frame Ellie's face with his hands, brushing the pads of his thumbs on her soft skin, so different than his own rough calluses.

"I remember this," he said and then brushed his lips against hers once, and then again, softly and sweetly, just as he had done in this very spot at his junior prom.

Ellie had closed her eyes the moment Buck leaned in. She knew he was going to kiss her even before she felt his warm breath against her lips.

Their first kiss, so many years ago, shared in the quiet privacy of the theater auditorium.

He had remembered.

And she remembered, as well. Emotions she'd thought she'd shelved long ago came rushing to the surface, flooding through her as if a dam had burst inside her.

As if twenty years hadn't passed.

As if this was their first kiss, all over again.

That moment, twenty-one years ago, had been the instant Ellie first knew Buck was the man for her, the one she wanted to spend her life with. She had been young and sentimental. It was their first date. She had hardly known Buck, certainly not enough to call what they had a relationship, much less something that would withstand the test of time.

It hadn't, of course.

Older and wiser now, Ellie knew how foolish it was to have banked her hopes on a first kiss. In her own defense, being raised in a small town, she'd watched year after year of Ferrell Ranger High School graduates marry each other and settle down right here in the area.

She hadn't given a thought to the fact that her life might be different. That was how it was, how it had always been, since Ferrell's founding in the late 1800s.

Many of the kids went off to college, of course, but

the majority of them went to the local university and came straight back to Ferrell upon graduation. Ellie's plans had included college, but they'd also included Buck. She knew he'd be working with horses, and they'd dreamed together about owning a ranch of their own.

So much for dreaming.

She'd learned the truth through the school of hard knocks. She wasn't that starry-eyed teenager anymore, but a pragmatist with a ministry to run. There was more to life than roping a cowboy husband.

She'd told herself the same things a thousand times, but for all that, right here in the present, one kiss from Buck changed everything. Ellie was just as vulnerable as she had been as a sixteen-year-old girl. Practicality and good common sense flew right out of her head.

A sense of panic surged through her. She had to get away from this situation *right now*. She needed time to gain some perspective, or she would lose herself in the moment, and who knew where that would lead?

Straight into another heartbreak. Nowhere she wanted to go in this lifetime.

Buck had left her before. What would stop him from doing so again?

Ellie broke away from Buck and hopped off the edge of the stage. Her heart wanted to trust him, but her head was screaming louder. Warning sirens were echoing inside her mind. Hadn't she learned anything the first time around?

"I'm sorry. I can't do this," she explained as she backed up the aisle, toward the theater doors.

Buck looked as stunned as she felt.

"What about the lights?" Buck called as Ellie

reached the doors. He was shielding his eyes with his hand, and Ellie was thankful for that, knowing from her own time onstage that Buck couldn't see her expression in the darkened theater.

"I'll get them later," she replied, pushing one of the doors open. "I've got to get back to the reunion. I have a date, who must think I've ditched him," she reminded Buck through a clenched chest and tight throat.

It was the only sensible course of action right now. The only way to salvage what was left of her heart. With immense effort, she set her mind on returning to Travis's side, where she belonged—at least for tonight.

Back to the safety and security of the friends she knew and loved.

Anywhere, as long as it was away from Buck.

Ellie found Travis leaning his shoulder against a far wall in the gym, close to the DJ and the loudspeakers. He was a handsome man, Ellie thought, with his neat dark brown hair and an immaculate gray business suit.

So why didn't her heart react when she saw him?

She wanted it to. If she could wish it true right now, she would. But if she were honest, she felt nothing except a sense of gratitude to Travis for his smile as she approached.

"I thought I'd lost you," he said, leaning down close to her ear to speak above the noise of the blaring speakers.

"I went for a walk," Ellie explained, flashing him an attempt at a smile, which felt more like a grimace.

"With Buck." It was a statement, not a question, and Ellie knew it.

She sighed. "Yes. With Buck. I'm really sorry,

Travis. I shouldn't have done that. I promise I won't leave your side for the rest of the night."

Travis stared down at her for a moment, his expression unreadable as he studied her face. Ellie didn't know what he was looking for, but she smiled for his benefit.

"How about you take a walk with me now?" Travis suggested after a long moment.

Ellie cringed inside. She wanted to stay in the relative safety of the gym, at least until she got her emotions back under control. But she had promised Travis she would stay at his side. If he wanted to take a walk, how could she refuse?

She nodded and tightened her grip on his arm.

"Lead the way," she said softly.

Ellie wasn't sure Travis could hear her voice over the noise, but her nod was enough to start him walking toward the exit doors, tucking her arm into the crook of his, with his free hand gently resting over hers. It was a comforting gesture, and one that Ellie appreciated.

Travis led her outside into the cool night air. After the stuffiness of the gym, the breeze felt good to Ellie, and she inhaled deeply, enjoying the fresh air.

"This is nice," she commented softly, giving Travis's arm a squeeze.

"And quiet," he replied, stopping at a bench under one of the trees. "The music in there was louder than I realized. Would you care to sit down?"

Ellie nodded and took a seat. Travis sat down next to her, but not as close as she would have expected. Instead, he sat at an angle, facing her.

"I think we should talk about Buck," Travis said without preamble.

Ellie tensed. Buck was the last subject she wanted to discuss. At least Travis could have eased into it with a little small talk, but as she searched his face, she could see he was in no mood for meaningless conversation. His smile was still in place, but his brown-eyed gaze was serious.

"I'd rather not," Ellie said, trying for a light tone but not quite succeeding.

"Maybe not," Travis said, "but we should."

"What about Buck?"

"He's obviously back in your life," Travis said, his smile twisting a little.

"Buck is *not* back in my life," she asserted, shaking her head vehemently.

Travis chuckled. "I think someone is in denial."

She shrugged. Travis was probably right. Just because she didn't want to think about Buck didn't mean he wasn't affecting every aspect of her life.

"I thought maybe the two of you were getting back together again when you left the gym together," he said softly.

A raw stab of guilt hit Ellie, and she felt even worse about herself than she had before. Travis was the innocent party here. He didn't deserve to be caught between whatever was *not* going on between her and Buck.

"I'm really sorry for leaving you like that," she apologized. "But I assure you Buck and I are not back together."

"Well, you should be."

Travis's statement shook Ellie to the core. She was glad she was sitting down. "How do you mean?"

Travis sighed. "Look, Ellie, I care a lot about you. You know I do."

"And I've met your thoughtfulness with blatant disregard," Ellie replied. "I'm so sorry."

Travis reached for Ellie's hand. "Please stop apologizing and hear me out."

"Okay." Ellie stared at Travis, waiting as he gathered his thoughts.

"I guess I've known for a long time our relationship wasn't going to work out."

"But—"

Travis held his free hand up, palm outward. "Please. Let me finish."

Ellie nodded miserably.

"If we were meant to be together, we'd be together. I've certainly pushed you on the subject enough. I think there's a reason you could never quite find it in your heart to commit to me."

Ellie looked away, unable to meet Travis's tender gaze. Maybe he was right. Maybe she did have commitment issues. If she did, Buck Redmond was certainly the cause of them.

"Buck didn't come back into town to renew a relationship with me," she stated firmly, feeling the nudge of pain her words brought with them.

"Perhaps not," Travis answered. "But you can't deny there's something still between the two of you."

She *wanted* to deny it. Oh, how she wanted to deny it. But she would be lying, and they both knew it.

"For a long time I hoped your feelings would

change toward me," Travis said. "You and I have always been good friends. But I've come to realize that's all that will ever be between us."

"I'm so sorry," Ellie said again.

Travis smiled wistfully. "Don't apologize. It's not like I figured that out tonight. I've known for some time. It's just that tonight I put all the pieces together and figured out why—what was really going on."

"I'm glad you've got it figured out," Ellie said with a deep sigh. "I'm sure I don't have a clue."

"Did it ever occur to you that God brought Buck back into your life for a reason?" Travis asked gently.

"What? To torment me?"

Travis chuckled. "To test your faith a little, maybe. But also, I think, to give you the desire of your heart."

"Buck Redmond is *not*…" Ellie started, and then her sentence drifted off into a prolonged silence.

Travis just smiled. "Buck is a proud man, Ellie. He may not even know he's still in love with you, but trust me, coming from another man, he is. Even if he's too stubborn to admit it."

Ellie immediately recalled Buck's kiss earlier that evening. He certainly hadn't been stubborn then, or unsure of what he wanted. She was the one who'd run out like her tail was on fire.

"I'm going to take you home, Ellie. I think you and Buck need to talk, to work this thing out between you."

"I guess you're right," she admitted grudgingly.

"I know I'm right. Don't let him walk away from you this time, Ellie. Make him stay."

Ellie squeezed Travis's hand. "Did anyone ever tell you what a wonderful man you are?"

Travis grinned. "Oh, women tell me that all the time. I have to fight them off with a stick, you know."

Ellie laughed. "I know you're just teasing, but I also know there are plenty of single women in Ferrell who would love to go out with you."

"Plenty?" Travis laughed with her. "Do you think?"

"I know," Ellie replied, giving Travis a hug. "And I know there's one special lady out there who God has planned just for you. She's going to be lucky to have you."

"Just be sure to tell Buck if he ever treats you wrong, he'll have to answer to me," Travis replied, still teasing but with just the slightest glimpse of truth in his gaze.

"I'll pass that threat along," she said, allowing the merest hint of hope to bloom in her heart. She only hoped she could follow through and confront Buck with her feelings. It might be the hardest thing she'd ever had to do.

Chapter Eight

Buck gave a frustrated huff as he adjusted the girth on his saddle. It wasn't the horse that was frustrating him. The thought of getting in the saddle and riding as far away from this whole situation as fast as possible was more than a little bit appealing to him right now.

Ellie was the one frustrating him.

For over a week now Ellie had avoided him, and he labored under no misapprehensions that it was some kind of accident. She no longer ate breakfast with Buck and Tyler, but was up and out on the ranch before they rose in the morning. She didn't join them for dinner, either, though she made the meals and had plates ready to go for everyone.

She didn't even suggest that Buck and Tyler attend church with her, as she had when they first arrived. Buck went, anyway, but Ellie was careful to avoid him even then.

Buck knew it was his fault. He'd scared her away when he'd kissed her. Scared her straight back into

Travis's arms, he imagined, though he hadn't seen anything firsthand. He hadn't returned to the reunion after Ellie had left him. He hadn't wanted to see Ellie and Travis together, and he hadn't been sure he could endure interacting with his old friends, so he'd headed back to the ranch, hoping Ellie would remember to turn off the stage lights, since he didn't know how to do it himself.

The gray skittered as the girth tightened, but Buck easily followed his gelding's movements. He had a sixth sense about horses. It was almost as if he knew what they were thinking, and he could easily anticipate Storm's next move and took one step backward as his horse shied against him.

If only he knew what *Ellie* was thinking. He sure couldn't anticipate her next move. He didn't have a clue.

He wasn't even so certain what *he* was going to do, apart from taking a nice, long head-clearing ride. Buck knew what he wanted from—*with*—Ellie. He just wasn't sure how to get it, or even if he could.

"Dad." Tyler raced out of the stable and over to the corral. He was smiling broadly and carrying a bridle threaded through his fingers.

Buck was glad to see his son smiling. Ever since coming back to Ferrell, Tyler had been nothing but cheerfulness and happy energy—a far cry from his old surly self. *Maybe the only good thing to come out of this time,* Buck mused.

"I brought this for you," Tyler said, holding the bridle at arm's length.

Buck smiled but shook his head. "I've already got a bridle here, son."

"I know," Tyler replied in a tone that Buck knew signaled his son thought his father was completely daft. "I saw you leave the stable."

"I didn't see you," Buck said, surprised.

"Yeah. I was in with the new colt."

"You're getting too attached, you know," Buck said in his gentlest voice. "When Ellie goes, she's taking the horses right along with her."

Tyler scowled, the expression Buck was used to seeing on his son's face. The boy carefully hung the bridle on the nearest fence post and faced his father off.

He was growing up, Buck realized, both physically and mentally. He guessed the boy would match his own six feet by the time he was out of his teenage years. Taller, even. Buck was certain Tyler would enjoy towering over his dad.

"I still don't get why Ellie has to leave. Why don't you like her, Dad?" Tyler demanded.

Buck sighed loudly and lifted his cowboy hat off his head in order to jam his fingers into his hair.

"I like Ellie just fine," he admitted gruffly. "It's just… Well, it's complicated."

Tyler folded his arms over his head and glowered at Buck. "Why do adults always say that every time they talk to kids, like we don't understand life or something? I'm twelve…almost thirteen years old, Dad, not a toddler."

Buck chuckled. "Tyler, *I* don't understand life right now. I'd give you an explanation if I had one."

"I do," Tyler said, still meeting his father's gaze fiercely, straight on.

"You do what?"

"Understand life. I know what's going on between you and Ellie."

"Really?" Buck said, arching an eyebrow. "Care to enlighten me, son?"

Tyler scoffed and shook his head. "You're in love with Ellie. And don't say you aren't, because I won't believe you."

Buck didn't move a muscle, but he felt like he'd been sucker punched in the gut. How had Tyler figured that one out? When Buck and Ellie were together— even in front of Tyler, though they both tried to watch themselves—they were constantly bickering about one thing or another. Buck hadn't made life easy for Ellie in *any* way since he'd come back to Ferrell.

But Tyler was right, of course.

Buck *was* in love with Ellie.

Maybe he hadn't put actual words to his feelings, but there it was, spelled out in black and white by his almost thirteen-year-old son, who was even now glaring at him, daring him to disagree with the analysis.

"And you know this how?" Buck said, stalling for time while he figured out what to say.

"I've seen the way you look at her when her back is turned," Tyler stated. "And I know you do stuff around here to help her out without her knowing about it."

"Hmm," was Buck's only response.

"If you just gave Ellie half a chance, Dad…" Tyler gestured with his hand, indicating that Buck could figure out the rest of the boy's sentence on his own.

Which he could. Maybe Ellie would love him, too—except that obviously wasn't the case, if her actions the past week were anything to go by. She wasn't just avoiding him; she was practically running in the other direction when she saw him coming.

"It's complicated," Buck said again.

Tyler's glare became even more intense. The boy shook his head and turned on his heel, away from Buck. His shoulders slumped, Buck's only indication of what his son must be feeling right now.

"Whatever," Tyler mumbled under his breath as he stalked back toward the stable.

"Son," Buck called.

Tyler froze in his tracks. Buck waited until the boy had turned to look at him before speaking.

"It's not a pat answer," Buck said softly. "It's the honest truth. I can't just waltz into the kitchen and ask Ellie to marry me, even if I wanted to."

"Why not?" Tyler asked with the mind of a grown man and the simple faith of a child. "Why not just ask her? It doesn't seem so complicated to me."

"There's…another man in her life," Buck offered, the first excuse to come to his mind.

"So?" Tyler challenged.

"So," Buck repeated, "I have to think about what Ellie wants right now."

"Yeah, right," Tyler said with the same hint of derision Buck had been used to in the past, but which had disappeared from Tyler's speech since he'd been at Ellie's. Now Tyler's surly attitude was suddenly back—in spades.

Buck sighed. "What's that supposed to mean?"

"Figure it out."

Buck met Tyler's glare head-on, challenging him with his best parental stare.

"Sorry," Tyler muttered, looking down at his feet and working the dirt with the toe of his cowboy boot, creating a small cloud of dust.

Tyler, apologizing? The boy really had changed in the month they'd been here.

"It's okay," Buck said instantly. "I know you weren't intentionally trying to be disrespectful."

Tyler shot him a wry grin.

"Okay," Buck hedged, "maybe you were. But I'll let it slide this time. I hear what you're saying."

"Good. 'Cause Ellie is a real special lady."

"Yeah, she is," Buck murmured. He shot his son a probing look. "Uh, how would you feel about that? If we were to stay here with Ellie, I mean."

Tyler laughed, his sullen mood gone just as quickly as it had come. Buck envied the ability of youth to just let things go and move forward with their lives. Buck had so much baggage, he wasn't sure he'd be able to do that.

"Do it, Dad," Tyler said, as if reading Buck's mind.

"Yeah, maybe," Buck said, evading the issue, not at all sure what he really was going to do. He'd blown his marriage to Julie. He'd hurt Ellie terribly when he'd left Ferrell. He didn't want to cause anyone any more pain, especially Ellie, and it seemed to Buck that pain followed him wherever he went.

"Okay. See you later," Tyler called, turning back toward the stable.

"You going somewhere?"

Tyler looked back, and Buck watched as the boy's face flushed red. "Out. With a girl."

Buck raised an eyebrow. "Hmm."

"Please, Dad. Don't go there," Tyler pleaded.

"I wasn't going to say anything," Buck assured him. "Except have fun. And maybe be home by...." Buck paused. This was the first time he'd had to lay out a curfew for the boy, and it wasn't something he'd thought about beforehand. "Uh, dinnertime, I guess?"

"Dad," Tyler said, his voice high and cajoling. "I'm almost thirteen."

"Right," Buck replied, pulling back his smile so his son wouldn't see. "Before dark, then."

Tyler shook his head like his father had just lost his mind, but he didn't argue. Instead he pulled his camel-colored cowboy hat off his head and combed his fingers through his smooth blond hair as he walked away.

Buck shook his head in amazement.

His son. With a girl.

Things were changing faster than Buck could keep up with, and here he was, contemplating sending his life straight into the ring with a raging bull.

Or rather, an angry woman. All things being equal, Buck would take the bull. He was crazy to even be thinking about staying on here at the ranch.

But he was.

Tyler was right. Things were at a complete impasse between Buck and Ellie, and they wouldn't be made right until the two of them talked.

Buck sighed and loosened the girth on the saddle. "Sorry, boy," he said to the horse. "Guess our ride has been indefinitely postponed."

The horse snorted, and Buck laughed. "I get enough attitude from my son, thank you very much."

Buck led Storm back to the stable and unsaddled him, mechanically giving him a quick rubdown and tossing some hay into the stall as he thought of the best way to approach Ellie. Should he tell her she could have the ranch first, or tell her he wanted to stay on to help her?

Or maybe he should start by telling her he wanted to spend the rest of his life trying to make it up to her for all the pain he'd caused. *Hmm.*

Still musing over his dilemma, Buck walked slowly back to the corral fence, where two bridles were hanging. He picked up the one he'd taken and slung it over his shoulder, then grabbed the bridle Tyler had brought to him.

He could see the bridle had been recently repaired, and from the quality of the work, Buck easily guessed Tyler had done the work himself. Buck wondered if Ellie had asked the boy to do it, or whether Tyler had taken his own initiative, which he seemed to be doing a lot of recently.

The answer was on the bridle itself. Freshly and carefully engraved on the leather that ran up the side of the horse's muzzle was the horse's name, Storm. On the other side were the initials MCTR.

McBride's Christian Therapy Ranch.

And that's what it would stay, Buck thought, gearing up his mind as if he were waiting to come out of the shoot on a bucking bronco. He wouldn't change a thing about how things were run around here and wouldn't even ask her to change the name of the ranch.

For just like the horse's name burned into the bridle, Ellie's name was firmly engraved in Buck's heart. But he knew there was one more thing he had to do before he approached Ellie, one more person he needed to get right with.

Buck opened the door to the birthing stall and spoke softly to the gangly little foal, still finding its legs. And then he slipped to his knees on the soft hay and did something he hadn't done in the twenty years since he'd left Ferrell.

He prayed.

Ellie was fitting new sheets onto a bed in one of the guest rooms when she felt Buck's presence in the doorway. She glanced back to find him leaning his shoulder casually against the door frame, a crooked half smile on his lips.

"Do you need something?" she asked, turning her gaze and her mind back to her work.

"Actually, yes," Buck drawled softly.

When he didn't say any more, Ellie straightened and turned, one hand massaging the small of her back. "I'm busy, Buck. What is it you want to tell me?"

"Do you have a second?"

Ellie shrugged. "Not really."

"You're going to make me beg?"

Ellie chuckled. "I *should* make you beg, but I won't. I really don't have much time, though. I have to finish planning Tyler's birthday party. There's still a lot to do, and it's only a couple of weeks away, you know."

Buck nodded crisply. "You always were the big party planner."

She chuckled. "Also, I have new clients coming in all the way from Kansas next week, and I still have to finish cleaning up their room and making sure all my wheelchair ramps are in working order."

"Kansas, huh? Word gets around, doesn't it? You

must be doing a great job here for people to come from out of state. You *are* doing a great job here," he corrected as he took Ellie by the elbow and led her from the room, down the hallway and into the kitchen, where he seated her at the table.

"The family decided to vacation in Texas," she explained. "Then they heard about the ranch and contacted me about coming here. Since their little boy is confined to a wheelchair, they'd like to give him the opportunity to experience a little bit of ranch life, things that might be out of his reach under normal circumstances."

Ellie gazed deep into Buck's bright green eyes and braced herself for the worst. This was when he was going to bring up how her therapy ranch was actually a tourist trap.

She didn't see any way to avoid the issue any longer. Still, it was worth a try, even if it was only a temporary diversion. "Where's Tyler?"

"Uh," murmured Buck, shaking his head. "Out. With a friend. With a *girlfriend*."

Ellie laughed. "Oh, that must be Sarah. She's Cindy Spencer's daughter. Very pretty."

"You knew about this?" Buck queried, sounding as equally demanding as he was bemused.

Ellie nodded. "Of course I did. I was there when he phoned and asked her out."

"And you didn't tell me this because…?"

"It wasn't like Tyler openly confided in me or anything," Ellie clarified. "I just happened to walk in on him when he was making the call. I think he was pretty embarrassed that I overheard his half of the conversation, but I didn't confront him on it."

"Or tell me about it."

Ellie nodded. "Or tell you. I figured when Tyler was ready to speak to you about his love life, he would do it himself."

"His *love* life?" Buck screeched. "My son has a love life? He's only twelve!"

"Thirteen in two weeks," Ellie reminded him gently. "He's growing up pretty fast, huh?"

"Hmm," Buck answered vaguely, and then his eyes narrowed on her. "You're trying to distract me, aren't you?"

"Is it working?"

"It *was* working," he said with a chuckle.

"What's so important?" Ellie asked, deciding to cut directly to the chase. She really didn't want to talk to him at all, but he was hardly giving her a choice in the matter.

Why postpone the inevitable?

Ellie knew what was coming, his real reason for wanting to talk to her, and it had nothing to do with Tyler's new girlfriend. In all honesty, she had been expecting this moment to come ever since the night of the reunion.

It was her own fault. She'd backed up when she should have moved forward. She'd run away from Buck instead of confronting her own feelings for him. In his mind, she must have firmly established that there was nothing between the two of them, and now Buck was going to kick her off the ranch.

She had no reason to think otherwise. Maybe if she'd followed Travis's advice and confronted Buck right after the reunion, things would have been different. But she hadn't moved fast enough, and things were what they were—the exact opposite of what she finally knew in her heart she really wanted, she realized.

Buck's frown didn't cheer her up any. He slid into the chair next to her, facing her. She noticed he didn't put any distance between them by straddling the back of the chair as he usually did. She felt a twinge of discomfort at their close proximity, and at the way Buck was looking at her, but outwardly she merely arched an eyebrow, reminding Buck he needed to answer her question.

What's so important?

"I think we should talk about what happened the other night at the reunion," Buck said, his tone firm, but quiet and neutral. "Don't you?"

He didn't give up anything in his expression, so Ellie had no idea what was running through his head.

"No, not really," she responded quietly after a moment's thought.

This time it was Buck who lifted an eyebrow.

"Okay, so we need to talk," Ellie said, mentally and emotionally preparing herself for the worst-case scenario. "When do you want me to move out?"

"Huh?" Buck asked, looking surprised and confused.

"My notice?" Ellie prompted. "Isn't that where you're going with this? You want me to get off your property. You've made that clear from the beginning. After what happened between us the other night at the reunion, I should think you'd want to be rid of me sooner rather than later, right?"

"Don't put words in my mouth," Buck demanded with steel in his voice. He scowled fiercely. "That wasn't what I was going to say at all."

Ellie thought back to what Travis had said to her regarding the mule-headed cowboy.

Don't let him walk away from you this time, Ellie. Make him stay.

If only it were that easy. But short of hog-tying him, Ellie couldn't think of how to keep him in her life. She couldn't force Buck to care for her, and if their kiss had meant anything, she hadn't seen it in the way Buck had been acting the past few days. He hadn't pursued her or tried kissing her again.

That she'd taken care to avoid him during that time was beside the point, wasn't it?

"Okay, then. What?" she asked with a sigh.

"You aren't going to make this easy on me, are you?" he growled quietly.

"Stop talking in circles, and say what you want to say," she countered.

"All right, then. I will. I'm not kicking you off the ranch, because I don't want you to leave the ranch. I've seen enough of the work you do here to know it counts for something. You really do have a ministry. It would be a shame for you to stop now, after all your hard work to make the ranch what it is." He swept in a breath, hesitating for just an instant. "Keep your work going, Ellie. Stay at the ranch."

"So when are you leaving?" While Ellie felt tremendous relief that he was letting her stay at the ranch, Buck's words wounded her more than she could have imagined.

Buck was going away again. This time for good.

"Leaving?" Buck looked dazed for a moment, but then he grinned. *Grinned.* "Actually, sugar, I wasn't planning on going anywhere."

True relief flooded Ellie's soul at that moment, though it took her a good minute to comprehend what Buck was saying. She immediately sent up a quick internal prayer thanking God for this miraculous change in events.

"So what do you think?" he asked when she continued her silent pondering.

"Let me get this straight," Ellie said, almost afraid to hope. "You are proposing we share the ranch together?"

"I am," Buck whispered hoarsely, enveloping her small hand in his large one, his green eyes luminous. "And I'm praying with all my heart that you'll give me the opportunity to make up for the past. I want to put all that behind us and start fresh."

Ellie was certain her jaw dropped in shock as Buck turned her toward him and pulled her into his arms.

"Buck?" she asked, her voice wavering.

"I know I messed up both our lives when I left Ferrell twenty years ago. I didn't realize just how bad off I was until I returned. I've spent my years being as surly and angry at God as Tyler has been with me— just a big, overgrown adolescent who didn't want to take responsibility for his own actions."

"Buck," Ellie repeated, softer now. Her heart was roaring so loudly, it was making her ears ring. She would have continued to speak, but Buck reached up and laid a gentle finger against her lips, stemming her flow of words before she could even begin.

"Just listen, please," he pleaded, his green eyes serious, but bright with a joy Ellie hadn't seen in him since before he'd left Ferrell in the first place. And as much as she loved Buck at that moment, she acknowledged that she alone couldn't have put such a spark in his eyes.

She prayed fervently for God's direction. *Fool me once, shame on you....*

"You, on the other hand," Buck continued, breaking into Ellie's internal prayer, "did *not* let circumstances dictate your faith. You moved forward with your life and have done something truly meaningful here at the ranch, helping all these children get past their trauma."

"I've had my share of heartache," she reminded him.

"I know," he replied gravely. "Don't you think I know I was the one who caused you pain?" Buck sighed. "I have a lot of regrets, Ellie. You and Tyler both deserve more than I offered. But I can't change the past. What I can do is look to the future—with you, if you'll let me."

"Buck," Ellie said for the third time in as many minutes. "Please. You've said enough."

He clamped his jaw shut, and Ellie saw the flash of disappointment in his eyes.

She squeezed his hand, reassuring him. "You don't have to say any more," she whispered, "because you had me at hello."

Buck smiled, a dazzling white-toothed grin, at her use of the old cliché. To Ellie, seeing the joy and happiness in his smile was like the dawn after a very dark night. She might have moved on with her life, as Buck had pointed out, but she realized now that deep in her heart she had always regarded Buck as her soul mate, even when he wasn't present in her life.

But still she was afraid. He had broken her heart once, she reminded herself. As much as she wanted to launch herself at him, the rational part of her mind was urging her to proceed with caution, lest this time be worse than the last.

She couldn't stand it if Buck left again, especially after what he'd just told her.

"I can't promise you anything," she whispered raggedly. "I want to trust you, but…" She let the rest of her thought dangle between them.

"I know I have a lot to make up for. I don't expect that we can just return to the way things were before I left twenty years ago. Things are different now. But you continue to amaze me, Ellie, with every breath I take. If it takes another twenty years, I'll earn your trust back."

She blinked away tears.

He gently framed her face with his large, callused hands. Slowly, giving her plenty of time to pull away, he leaned in to her, tipping his head, his mouth hovering over hers, taking his own sweet time but stopping painfully shy of sealing their conversation with a kiss.

"Come here, cowboy." Impatiently, Ellie reached for the collar of his black Western shirt and pulled him closer so their lips could finally meet. He kissed her lightly for a moment, then deeply.

"Dad?"

Ellie hazily recognized the disembodied voice, but it didn't quite register for a moment. Her head was swimming with emotion, and her heart was thrumming in her ears.

"Ellie!"

This time the voice was like a jolt of electricity. Ellie jumped back, completely out of Buck's arms, and turned guiltily to face Buck's son, who was standing in the doorway, with a stunned expression on his face. Before she could object, Buck stepped behind Ellie and placed reassuring hands on her shoulders.

"Hello, son," Buck said smoothly. "Back so soon?"

Tyler nodded, still looking bemused. "I—I forgot my wallet in my room," he stammered.

"I can explain," Ellie said, desperately seeking words that really *would* explain what had just happened between Tyler's father and her. She realized belatedly how this must appear to the boy, walking in on his father like that, and she hurried to clarify what Tyler had seen. "I—I…"

She didn't have time to finish whatever convoluted sentence would have escaped her lips. Tyler, smiling with such joy that Ellie's heart did another backflip, raised his fist straight up in the air and pulled it back down to his side.

"All *right!*"

Chapter Nine

The next two weeks went by in a flash as Buck and Ellie planned the future of their ranch together. They decided to keep this new turn of events between the two of them until Tyler's birthday, hoping it would be a great surprise for him.

Ellie had mentioned to Buck how a national organization for therapy ranches helped breeders and ranchers connect, and Buck was off and running with ideas on how to use the ranch to breed and train stock for other therapy ranches, in addition to helping run Ellie's ranch.

His and Ellie's ranch.

Buck sure liked the sound of that. He sighed contentedly and took in a deep breath of fresh morning air. Peace flooded his soul, unlike anything he'd ever felt before. He had Ellie, his son, their ranch. And though he knew he had a lot of work ahead of him to get Ellie to trust him again, for the first time in twenty years, Buck felt truly blessed by God.

"Are you coming?" Tyler let the screen door slam as he dashed out onto the back porch, breaking into Buck's reverie with the skittishness of a green-broke horse.

Buck smiled at his son, slowly stretching to work the kinks out of his shoulders. He took his time, enjoying the sight of Tyler squirming in impatience.

"Do you need me?" he teased, laughing as he watched Tyler's expression turn from excitement to exasperation.

Tyler rolled his eyes. "*I* don't need you. But I think Ellie is going to pitch a royal fit if you don't get in there and help her with the decorations."

"What? You can't blow up balloons?" Buck winked to show he was still teasing.

"I could if Ellie would let me," Tyler immediately retorted. "She won't let me do anything. And she keeps calling me the birthday boy. Dad, you've got to make her stop."

"I don't know if I can do that, son. You know how stubborn Ellie is when she gets something into her head." Buck laughed heartily. It felt so good to be able to verbally fence with his son and not have it turn into a full-blown argument.

He and Tyler were definitely benefiting from the stabilizing influence Ellie had on both of them. Ever since they had arrived at the ranch, she had gone to a great deal of trouble to make them both feel like they were *home,* from cooking their meals to playing mother hen. From the extraordinary grin lining his son's expression, Buck thought Ellie was definitely making progress.

"If she calls me birthday boy in front of my friends…" Tyler let the sentence dangle.

"Especially Sarah?" Buck guessed.

Tyler's face reddened under his father's close scrutiny. "Dad," he pleaded, "it's bad enough to have Ellie hovering over me. Don't embarrass me in front of Sarah."

Buck laughed. "Me? I'd never do that to you."

Tyler didn't look so sure about that, but he laughed, anyway. "Ellie's waiting for you."

Buck shook his head. "Don't remind me. Why did I say I would help with this again?"

Tyler opened his mouth to speak, but Buck brought him up short.

"Oh, yeah," Buck continued. "It's your thirteenth birthday. You're officially a teenager." He chucked his son in the arm. "You're growing like a weed, you know that? And you really help out around here—when Ellie lets you," he said with a laugh. "I'm proud of you, Tyler."

Tyler's face reddened even more, if that were possible.

"Whatever," Tyler mumbled as he turned on his heel and raced back inside, but Buck could tell his son was pleased by the compliment. And Buck really meant it, too.

Buck followed Tyler inside the ranch house and, seeing no sign of his son, looked for Ellie.

He found her in the kitchen, singing a cheerful praise song as she wrapped the yellow cake in smooth chocolate frosting. It was enough to make Buck's mouth water. It had been a long time since he'd had homemade cake.

"I forgot how much I love your voice," he said huskily as he turned a chair around and straddled it. "I think that was the first thing I noticed about you."

Ellie smiled but didn't look away from her cake. "Did you get the extra ice cream from the store like I asked you to?" she queried lightly.

"Two gallons of Neapolitan ice cream, just as instructed, ma'am," he replied in the same airy tone. "Although if you ask me, I think that's a bit of an overkill. How many kids did you say were coming to this party?"

"Twenty," she answered crisply, then laughed. "And trust me—they'll devour that whole two gallons of ice cream. Teenagers, remember?"

Buck groaned. "Don't remind me. I can't believe Tyler is growing up so fast."

"They do that, don't they?"

"Seems like he's grown a lot since we first got here," Buck commented thoughtfully.

"At least an inch or two."

"No, I meant *grown up*. Tyler never used to respect authority, and he hated helping out around the ranch, except with the horses, and only when I didn't nag him to do it. Now he's practically pulling his own weight around here, and I never have to say a word to him. You're a wonderful influence on the boy."

"I think it helps that his father isn't so strung up anymore," she replied. "You've finally learned what it means to rest and relax—not that you don't do a lot around here to help, as well," she added hastily.

Buck laughed. "If that's the back door to a compliment, I accept."

"Good," she said, glancing at him. Her gaze said what she didn't say aloud, that she wanted to drop the subject before he embarrassed her again. "You haven't finished decorating the living room."

Buck held his hands up. "Guilty as charged. I thought I'd step out and get a breath of fresh air first."

"Not that you need it to blow up those balloons," she teased, a twinkle in her violet eyes.

"Okay, so I know *that* wasn't a compliment. Are you implying I'm full of hot air?"

"I didn't say a word," she protested.

"Hmm," he answered vaguely, but he shoved himself out of the chair and headed for the living room, where a pile of decorations lay on the coffee table.

After an hour of stringing balloons, twirling and taping crepe paper and setting the dining-room table, Buck was finally finished with his chores. And it was a good thing, too. Moments later the first of Tyler's guests arrived, some of them even coming by bus from Silverdale.

Soon the ranch house was filled with rowdy boys and giggling girls. Buck made it a point to stay out of the middle of the ruckus, choosing to lean his shoulder on a far wall and watch the scene from across the room.

Unlike Buck, Ellie loved parties, and she was especially happy to be throwing Tyler his birthday bash. She thrived right in the middle of all the chaos as she served her teenage guests a frothy green punch. She couldn't remember ever feeling happier, she thought as another wave of joy washed over her.

Tyler was flushed and beaming and grinning widely, and that was all Ellie could wish for.

"Hello," she called to the group at large. It took a good minute and a lot of gesturing to get everyone's attention, as the kids were spread out all over both the living and dining rooms. "Let's get this party rolling," she suggested with a hoot.

Her announcement led to a cacophony of voices cheering and yelling. Poor Tyler would be black and blue from all the friendly punches and back slaps the boys were giving him.

"Gifts or cake first?" she asked the excited crowd.

"Gifts, gifts, gifts," the boys chanted in unison, their voices in a lower octave. The girls just giggled.

"Okay, then," Ellie answered with a laugh. "Gifts it is. Tyler, please be seated here," she said, gesturing to a chair set in the middle of the room. "That way everyone can see you as you open your presents."

She refrained from calling him the birthday boy, but just barely. Ellie was as excited as the kids to be a part of this. Moment by moment she was woven more deeply into the fabric of Buck and Tyler's life.

As Tyler started tearing into his presents, Ellie suddenly felt Buck's presence nearby. Standing behind her, he wrapped his arms around her waist and leaned in close to her ear.

"What did you get him?" Buck whispered, his smooth, deep voice sending velvet shivers down her spine.

"Wait and see," she teased.

"Not even a little hint?"

She chuckled. "Okay. A mode of transportation," she answered, being as vague as possible.

"What?" Buck exclaimed. He groaned. "Please don't tell me you got him a car."

"I didn't get him a car. He's only thirteen. Besides, I can't afford to buy him a car."

"Good point," Buck answered.

Ellie and Buck both quieted as Tyler picked up the

card Ellie had given him. Moments later he was cheering at the top of his lungs. "All *right!*"

Ellie felt Buck lean in closer, trying to see what she had given the boy. She laughed again. "It's a picture."

"Of what?"

Tyler turned to his father. "Look, Dad. It's a picture of the new colt."

Ellie couldn't smile any wider. "Which I purposefully didn't name," she indicated. "He's all yours. Name him, raise him and train him. I know you'll do a great job. You're as good a cowboy as your dad is. Happy birthday, Tyler."

"Thanks, Ellie," Tyler said, his voice cracking. "This is the best birthday party *ever.*"

From behind her, Buck groaned again, though he didn't let go of Ellie's waist.

"What is it?" Ellie queried.

"This is Tyler's *only* birthday party ever," he said, his voice lined with regret. "At least probably that he can remember. His mother used to throw parties. That just wasn't my forte, you know?"

"I know," Ellie answered simply and compassionately. "And I think Tyler does, as well."

"All I can say is it's a good thing he has you now," Buck answered. He sounded like he was a little choked up, and Ellie wondered at his spontaneous burst of emotion.

"What did you get him?" Ellie asked, smoothly changing the subject as she peered over the heads of some of the teenagers, trying to see the gift Tyler was opening next.

Buck laughed. "Let's just say it goes perfectly with

your present. We couldn't have done it better if we had planned it this way."

"Is that so?" Ellie now saw what Buck meant as Tyler opened Buck's gift to him, a new bridle and a leather-burning kit.

"So you can mark all the bridles in the stable," Buck explained, nodding at the leather-burning kit. "I saw what you did with Storm's bridle, and I really liked it."

Tyler grinned. "Thanks, Dad."

Ellie placed her hand over Buck's and squeezed. Father and son were growing closer by the day.

"I can't wait to tell Tyler that you guys are going to stay on here at the ranch," Ellie murmured. "Or do you think we should wait until later to tell him?"

"No way," Buck replied. "I can't wait. I don't want to, either. We're telling him tonight, like we planned. You know he'll be happy for us."

"I hope so."

"He's rooting for us," Buck assured her. "Trust me on this. He is one smart kid."

Ellie grinned. "Not *so* much a kid anymore," she teased, and then her expression softened in tune with her heart. "I can't believe how much I love that boy."

Buck brushed her hair back and kissed her softly on the cheek, his eyes shining an incandescent green.

By this time Tyler was sitting among a pile of opened presents and, more important, Ellie thought, in the middle of a crowd of new friends. She had the feeling Tyler was going to like growing up in Ferrell as much as she had. And as Buck had—at least until he'd tangled with his mother and the town.

"Let's get the cake," Ellie whispered to Buck. He

nodded and followed her to the kitchen, where she planted thirteen candles deep into the chocolate frosting while Buck stood behind her, nuzzling her neck.

"Cut that out," she whispered with a giggle. "One of the kids might see."

"Let them," Buck growled, but he released his hold on her—at least partway. His arm was still firmly draped over her shoulder, and Ellie leaned into his warmth. "Let's do this thing," he said, winking at Ellie before he released her completely so he could carefully light the candles with a match.

Buck had informed Ellie soon after they met that he was tone-deaf, and Ellie had never heard him sing before, so she was surprised when Buck joined in a rowdy rendition of the happy birthday song. Even more surprising was Buck's voice, a smooth, lovely baritone.

And he could follow a tune.

So much for being tone-deaf. Ellie wondered how many other discoveries she was going to make about Buck over the coming years. He was surprising her at every turn, from the sound of his singing voice to the shirt he was wearing today, a bright green that matched his eyes.

Ellie had bought it for him the day after the reunion and had nonchalantly left it hanging in his closet. Up until today she didn't know if he'd so much as noticed it was there, and she experienced a wave of elation that he was wearing it now, just for her.

She had time to learn all about Buck and Tyler— the rest of their lives together, she hoped.

At the moment all she could hear was laughter. Buck's

laughter. Tyler's laughter. Joy swirled in her chest, ballooning into her head and making her a little bit dizzy.

She quickly cut slices of the cake and passed them to the hungry teens as Buck scooped the ice cream. They worked quietly together, not needing to speak. Ellie caught him smiling down at her several times.

"You were right," Buck said, breaking the silence— *at least between the two of them,* Ellie thought, pleased by the clamor Tyler's friends were making—as he finished off the first gallon of Neapolitan and rinsed out the plastic tub before tossing it in the recycle bin. "We did need two gallons."

"Told you so," she teased.

"When do I get to sample some of that great-looking homemade cake of yours?" he inquired, waggling his eyebrows. "I barely restrained myself from snagging a piece before the party began. If it's anywhere near as delicious as it looks…"

Buck's sentence trailed off as Ellie cut off a small corner of the cake and lifted it to Buck's mouth.

"Practicing?" Buck teased through a mouthful of cake.

It was the words he didn't say that threw her. Ellie choked up on her own bite of cake and coughed violently. Buck patted her awkwardly on the back. Commitment was still a huge issue between them, and Ellie was positive Buck, of all people, would be gun-shy about getting married.

At that moment someone knocked sharply and rapidly on the front door.

"I'll get it," Ellie said promptly, relieved to have something physical to do, something to get her away from Buck for a moment. She needed to think, to regain her equilibrium after what he'd just hinted at. "It's probably another one of Tyler's friends," she muttered. "I didn't ever get a head count. Did you?"

Buck shook his head. "Whoever it is at the door probably rang the bell several times. I don't know about you, but I can't hear a thing over this ruckus."

Ellie smiled. "Isn't it wonderful?"

Buck cupped Ellie's face for a quick, appreciative kiss. Part of her wanted to pull away, but that was immediately overridden by the pressure of Buck's warm, soft lips and gentle touch. "Yeah, sugar. It is wonderful."

At length Ellie put her palms on Buck's chest and pushed him away. "I have to get the door, Buck." Her voice caught in her throat and came out raspy.

He chuckled. "Yeah. Right. The door." Reluctantly he gave way and allowed Ellie to squirm out of his embrace.

Head still spinning, she weaved her way through the teenagers crammed in the living room and toward the front door.

Good thing she wasn't claustrophobic, she thought with a grin. "Excuse me. Pardon me. Excuse me," she quipped, edging closer toward the door with each step. "Welcome," she said as she swung the front door open wide and smiled at the newcomer. "Buck and Tyler and I are glad you could make it today."

To her surprise, it wasn't a teenager on the other side of the door. It was a beautiful woman with sparkling blue eyes and blunt-cut, short blond hair. Ellie didn't recognize the lady and wondered if she was new in town.

"Oh, I'm sorry," Ellie apologized immediately. "I thought you would be one of Tyler's friends. Are you somebody's mother? Good luck finding them in this wild horde."

The woman's gaze widened and she shook her head. "I'm Tyler's…"

"Julie," came Buck's surprised voice from directly behind Ellie. "What are you doing here?"

Chapter Ten

Buck was so stunned, he couldn't breath. He couldn't say another word. Through a murky haze of surprise, he wondered if his heart was even beating.

Ellie glanced back at him. All the color drained from her face as she repeated what Buck had just said. "Julie?"

The woman continued to stand on the doorstep, her smile faltering. She made no move to enter the house, which was just as well, Buck thought, shock and anger warring for prominence in his chest. He should just toss her out again. How dare she show up at their son's birthday party?

Their son.

That biological fact couldn't be denied. Buck didn't know what to do. He wanted to demand that Julie turn right around and return to whatever rock she'd crawled out from under, but he didn't want to make a scene. Not at Tyler's birthday party. A sledge-hammer pounded relentlessly at his temple as he fought to contain the anger simmering just under the surface, which was threatening to erupt at any moment now.

Ellie seemed to snap out of it at that moment. "Please, come in," she said, gesturing for Julie to enter the house. "It's Tyler's thirteenth birthday today."

"I know," said Julie, pinching her lips and looking, Buck thought, very much like she might burst into tears. Julie always had been somewhat of a spoiled drama queen. Apparently the years hadn't changed her a bit.

Julie hesitated on the doorstep, looking from Buck to Ellie and back to Buck again. Her eyes widened slightly. "I can come back another time," she said, her voice cracking.

Buck vehemently shook his head. "No. You can't. You think you can just show up—"

Ellie stopped the flow of Buck's angry words with a calming palm to his chest. "Buck. Now is not the time or place. Let her come in."

Buck glared at Julie but backed away, allowing her to enter the ranch house. "I don't think this is a good idea," he said softly to Ellie, but loud enough that Julie could hear it.

"Maybe not," Ellie agreed quietly, for Buck's ears only. "But what choice do we have? If you make a scene now, it will ruin Tyler's party."

Buck blew out a frustrated breath. He wanted to scream. At Julie.

"I know you're right," he growled, clenching and unclenching his fists in a vain attempt to reel in his anger. "She just caught me off guard."

"That's the understatement of the century," Ellie

whispered, squeezing Buck's arm before turning to their new guest. "Would you care for a piece of cake, Julie?"

Buck could tell Ellie was as off-kilter as he was. He felt her fingers shaking where they gripped his arm, though she kept her expression polite and neutral. If Julie's sudden appearance had stunned him, he could only imagine how Ellie felt at suddenly and unexpectedly meeting his ex-wife. He wanted to sweep Ellie away, to reassure her that nothing had changed.

But it had. The moment Ellie had opened the front door to Julie, it had. And there was no getting around it.

"She doesn't want a piece of cake." Buck answered for Julie, his eyes narrowing on the unsolicited visitor.

"No, thank you," Julie agreed.

"Let's take this into the kitchen," he suggested through a clenched jaw.

And get it over with, he added mentally.

The sooner he talked to Julie, the sooner she would be gone—with Tyler none the wiser, Buck hoped, although he imagined *Julie* had different plans in mind.

Not that he cared what Julie's plans were. She wasn't going to get the chance to act on them.

"You and Julie go," Ellie prompted. "I'll stay out here and oversee the party."

"Ellie," Buck ground out.

Ellie laid a palm on his chest. "This is between the two of you, don't you think?"

Buck blew out another breath. He struggled to remain calm on the outside when he was shaking with fury on the inside.

"I guess. She won't be staying long," he promised,

laying his hand over Ellie's soft fingers and giving them a light squeeze.

"I understand if you need some time," Ellie whispered back to him.

"I *don't* need time," he snapped, then dragged in a breath through his teeth. "I'm sorry. I don't mean to be taking my frustration out on you."

"I know," was Ellie's simple response.

Buck nodded at Julie and gestured toward the kitchen. "We can talk in here."

"Thank you," was all Julie said.

Buck knew the exact second Julie spotted Tyler, for she froze in place, nothing moving except her shoulders, which shuddered repeatedly. Buck couldn't see her face and therefore didn't have any idea how she was taking this. All he knew was he couldn't let her speak to Tyler.

Not now.

Preferably not ever.

He strode forward, placing his hand on the small of her back and propelling her away from Tyler as quickly as possible. Buck maneuvered his ex-wife into the kitchen, wishing there was a door between the kitchen and dining room so he and Julie could talk in private without a chance of being overheard.

"Maybe we should take a walk outside," he suggested in a low voice.

Julie nodded. "That's a good idea."

Buck opened the back door and let Julie go first. She didn't speak as they ambled down the hill, toward the stable. He bit his lip against the silence until he could no longer stand it.

"Why are you here?" he demanded, reaching for Julie's elbow and hauling her to a stop.

"I needed to see Tyler," she explained, her voice rough and tears marking the corners of her eyes.

Buck shook his head. "Of all the nerve. Ten years go by and suddenly you need to see your son?"

Julie held up both hands in an apologetic gesture. "I know. I've treated you both abominably."

"I'll say," Buck growled.

"I have no excuse for my actions, except that I was young and stupid."

"Not good enough."

"I know," she replied, breaking her gaze from Buck and softly swirling the dirt at her feet with the toe of one sneaker. "That's why I'm here."

"To what? Apologize? Julie, there is nothing you can say to me that will make any difference."

"I figured you'd probably react this way," she said softly and apologetically.

"Really?" Buck crossed his arms over his chest. "You figured, huh? What was your first clue?"

"I don't blame you for being angry."

"Angry?" Buck huffed. "Lady, I passed *angry* years ago. I don't feel anything for you now."

"I didn't expect you to."

"Too much time has passed. You never called, never wrote. You just disappeared. *You deserted your own son!*"

"Like I said before, no excuses." Julie's voice remained calm, if wavering, and she didn't quite meet Buck's gaze. "I just wanted to see Tyler."

"Well, you've seen him," Buck ground out. "Now get out of here and go back to wherever it is you came from."

"I—I had hoped to talk to him," Julie stammered, turning her back on Buck and taking a couple of steps away from him—out of his reach, he imagined.

"Not a chance," Buck said fervently. "I'm not going to let you hurt him any more."

Julie shook her head. "I won't tell him I'm his mother," she insisted. "I just want to speak with him for a few minutes. Is that too much to ask?"

"Frankly, yes."

"Okay."

That one quietly spoken word sent a wave of guilt washing over Buck.

Guilt!

What did he have to feel guilty about?

She was the one who had left, who had broken their son's heart. He was only looking out for the welfare of his son by sending Julie away, wasn't he?

Suddenly he wasn't so sure. Was he really looking out for Tyler's best interests, or was it himself he was worried about? He was certainly worried about how Ellie would take all this; their relationship was hanging by the most tenuous of threads. Something like this could make it snap entirely, though he had to admit, however grudgingly, that Julie was carrying herself with a reserved poise that didn't appear overtly threatening.

He'd lost his perspective the moment Julie showed up on the doorstep. He wished he had stayed at Ellie's side and not gone off on his own with Julie, even if Ellie had been the one to suggest that he and Julie should be alone to talk. Buck began to pray fervently under his breath, asking for God to intervene in what could turn into a blowout situation for everyone concerned, especially if Buck didn't handle it right.

"We have to go back to the house," he said hoarsely, then cleared his throat.

Julie raised her eyebrows, but nodded complacently. "I know you've already made up your mind about me," she said softly. "But I hope you'll reconsider."

Buck highly doubted that would happen, but at the end of the day, Julie was still Tyler's biological mother. She had no legal rights to the boy, Buck had seen to that, but he could understand her wanting to see Tyler. *Ten years ago, maybe.*

Why had Julie shown up now, just when things were finally starting to fall into place in his life? For the first time in forever he'd been happy, but that had blown up in his face the moment Julie arrived.

As he entered the ranch house, Julie hard on his heels, Buck realized he hadn't even properly introduced Ellie and Julie. He'd been so taken aback by Julie's sudden arrival, he hadn't thought of the formalities. Clearly Ellie had figured it out on her own, though, and right now Buck needed her help—an outside, though not totally unbiased, perspective.

"Wait here," he told Julie as soon as they entered the kitchen. Buck made his way back out to the living room, where he found Ellie quietly standing by the punch bowl, her arms wrapped in front of her and a wistful look on her face.

"I need your help," he stated without preamble as he approached Ellie.

"Did you two work things out already?" she asked, sounding surprised.

"Not exactly," Buck growled.

Not even close.

He took Ellie's hand and half dragged her into the kitchen. He could understand, her reluctance to interfere. He would feel the same way in her position. The fact of the matter was, if he could see any way to avoid this conflict entirely, he would definitely be the first one crowding out that door.

"Ellie, this is my ex-wife, Julie," he said, wrapping a protective arm around Ellie's waist. He couldn't say he was really surprised when Ellie immediately stepped out of his reach, but it still hurt. He cleared his throat.

"I'm sorry, Julie," he continued, doing his best to be polite. "I don't know what last name you go by now. Julie, this is, er, my friend Ellie McBride." He had wanted to introduce her as something more than just a friend, but he wasn't sure if Ellie was ready for that, given the circumstances.

Julie gave what Buck had to admit appeared to be a genuine smile and held out her hand to Ellie.

"It's nice to meet you," they said simultaneously. It might have been humorous were the situation not as tense and high-strung as it was.

Buck grimaced. Hadn't he put Ellie through enough? Yet she appeared to be taking this well enough. His chest clenching painfully, he plunged forward. "Julie is here to see Tyler," he explained roughly, jamming his fingers into his hair.

"I see," Ellie said, when she clearly did not.

"I just want to talk to him," Julie added, tacking her comment onto the back of Buck's statement. "I have no intention of telling him who I am. Can you understand that?"

Ellie shook her head. "No. Not really. Not now."

Buck's heart swelled as Ellie took on the role of protector to Tyler, showing her love for the boy more clearly than Buck could ever have imagined.

"Look, I understand how you both must feel." Julie gestured with both hands.

"Do you?" Buck asked curtly and then clamped his mouth shut again.

Hadn't he changed at all, grown at all, in his time here at the ranch with Ellie? Was he the same gruff man he'd been when he came back to Ferrell? Hadn't his new relationship with God made *any* difference in his life?

With a quick prayer, he bolstered his defenses, trying to shut out his natural emotional response, the stab of betrayal he felt every time he looked into Julie's eyes. Buck fought to be the better man here and not purposefully antagonize Julie. That wouldn't solve anything.

"I can't say enough how sorry I am for my past actions," Julie continued.

Ellie crossed her arms and stepped back closer to Buck's side, creating what Buck thought might be a mental barricade against anything Julie might say or do. Buck wanted to wrap Ellie in his arms and protect her from all this, but he knew she wouldn't accept his reassurance. Not now.

Ellie didn't know what to think—in fact, she could barely think at all with the sea of emotions enveloping her. She tried to pray but felt as if her words were bouncing off the ceiling and coming right back at her.

How could God have allowed this to happen?

Why now?

She gazed at Buck, empathizing with the anger and bewilderment written all over his expression. His jaw was tight, and Ellie knew he was desperately trying to control himself, keep a hold on his quick temper. She admired him for that, at least.

But it wasn't fair for Buck to bring her into the middle of this situation. She was the last person on earth who could offer any kind of impartiality. This was between Buck and Julie and, Ellie thought, hopefully nobody else—especially Tyler. The whole thing was a sure heartbreak for the boy any way Ellie looked at it.

She could hardly stand to look at the pain in *Buck's* face. She didn't know how she could possibly watch *Tyler* experience one more disappointment in his life, especially something this major. Yet here Julie was, and Ellie knew deep down she could not send the woman away as abruptly as she wished.

Ellie closed her eyes for a moment and took an intense, calming breath. Whether she liked or not, she *had* been thrust into the middle of this situation between Buck and his ex-wife, and had no choice now but to mediate the best she could and hope for a miracle.

There was a deafening silence in her head and heart, where Ellie wanted immediate—and definitive—answers. She sighed and brushed her fingers back through her hair.

"Okay, Julie. I think you'd better stay the night," Ellie said at last.

"What? No," Buck answered for his ex-wife before Julie could so much as say a word.

Ellie glanced over her shoulder to see Buck glowering at Julie. Julie stared straight back at Buck, looking decidedly uncomfortable as she clasped her hands in front of her. Ellie felt the tension in the air, as tangible as a room full of invisible gas just waiting for a single spark to make it blow up in flames.

"It only makes sense, Buck," Ellie explained. "We aren't going to work this out in the next fifteen minutes, and Tyler's birthday party is winding down soon."

"I don't have to stay here," Julie inserted tentatively. "I'll just check in to a motel in town."

Ellie attempted to smile but was convinced it was little more than a grimace. "The county fair is going on. There are only two motels in Ferrell, and I'm pretty sure they are booked solid."

"There's one in Houston," Buck suggested through gritted teeth. "Or Dallas."

Ellie whirled on him. "Be reasonable, Buck. It's too late in the day to send her off to Dallas or Houston. Besides, this is only temporary. Right, Julie?"

Holding her breath, Ellie looked to Julie for conformation. She was relieved when the woman nodded her affirmation.

Only temporary.

Then why did it feel so incredibly permanent?

At length, Buck shrugged his assent. "I still think it's a bad idea, but it's your ranch, Ellie."

What?

Her ranch?

What had happened to *their* ranch?

Ellie scowled at Buck. "It's settled, then. Julie, let me show you to your room. You can have dinner with us. Tyler will be there. But I warn you, if you hurt that boy, you'll be answering to me. Do you understand?"

Julie nodded vigorously, her eyes wide in apparent shock and distress.

"Hmm," Buck muttered, crossing his arms and staring at Ellie. She wanted to squirm under his gaze, but she squared her shoulders, determined to see this through.

"And you," Ellie continued, using her index finger to poke Buck square in the middle of his chest. "You stay right where you are. We need to talk."

Buck opened his mouth as if he were about to say something, then apparently thought better of it and clamped his lips together. Whatever he'd been about to say would have to wait.

Since she'd instructed Buck to wait for her in the kitchen, Ellie herself went outside and took the suitcase from the backseat of Julie's brand-new white SUV and settled her in one of the guest bedrooms. Fortunately Ellie had an extra guest bedroom already made up, so it didn't take long to settle Buck's ex-wife in.

Ellie had turned and was heading back to the kitchen, where Buck waited, when she suddenly whirled back to face Julie. As an afterthought, she informed Julie that dinner would be served promptly at seven that evening.

Ellie passed through the living room on her way back to the kitchen, taking a moment to speak with Tyler. Most of his friends had gone, with only a few rowdy boys left over. She suggested they go look at Tyler's present in the stable, the new foal, and try to pick out a name for him.

If Tyler suspected anything was amiss, or had even

noticed Julie's untimely arrival, he didn't show it. Ellie breathed a sigh of relief when the boys scrambled out the door. It was enough that she had to confront Buck without worrying about Tyler.

"I'm sorry," Buck said the moment Ellie entered the kitchen.

"You should be."

"I know that wasn't fair, putting you in the middle of this. But I honestly didn't know what else to do."

"Uh, handle it yourself?" Ellie suggested grimly.

Buck shrugged. "I tried. But I was losing my perspective, Ellie. I need your help."

He sounded so genuine, Ellie couldn't help but be touched by his plea, yet her heart was torn. Did he really think it would help for her to get in between him and his ex?

She stared down at her hands for a moment, and her mind wandered back to when Mama Esther was still alive. Grief struck her anew.

Buck's mom would have known what to do. She had had a remarkable sense about people and had been gifted in her ability to discern what they were really about.

Ellie had no clue. She just knew it wasn't right.

"Listen, Buck," she began hesitantly, not quite meeting Buck's gaze. "I don't think we should risk telling Tyler about our plans right now. It's definitely not the appropriate time to rock his world."

"Not even for the good?" Buck whispered. "I would think good news would be welcome about now. I think it would make him happy to hear of our plans for the ranch."

"I don't think we should be *making* any plans right now. Not with everything so up in the air."

"What?" Buck frowned, his forehead creasing ominously. "Nothing is up in the air, Ellie. Nothing has changed. Trust me on this."

Trust him. That was the problem. Ellie still wasn't sure she could. And now, with Julie back, who knew what would happen? She knew only that she needed to guard her heart.

"Don't give up on me," he whispered raggedly. He reached for her hands. "I get what's going on here. You're taking responsibility for something that is not your problem."

"That's exactly it, Buck," Ellie said, tears now flowing down her cheeks. "It *isn't* my problem. This is between you and Julie. You can't go forward with your life with me until you've put the past truly to rest."

Buck sighed and nodded, though he did not let go of her hands. "I know things seem pretty crazy right now, but know this. I will never let you go again. Never."

Chapter Eleven

To Buck's chagrin, Tyler chattered all the way through dinner. Ellie had introduced Julie to Tyler as merely a guest, saying no more about it than that. The only picture Tyler had of his mother was of her holding him when he was a newborn. Time and stress had taken their toll on Julie, and she now hardly resembled the young, carefree woman in the faded photograph. The boy appeared to have taken Ellie's word at face value, despite the fact that Julie had no children with her.

Fortunately, Tyler seemed distracted by the success of his first real birthday party—at least the first one that the boy would remember. He was practically bubbling over about the foal Ellie had given him for a present.

"I've decided to call him Jet," Tyler explained to Ellie between bites of food. "Him being black and all."

Unable to find his own appetite, Buck pushed his plate away. Despite Ellie's prowess in the kitchen, nothing tasted good. Buck couldn't taste anything at all.

He kept staring at Julie, feeling as tense as a large

cat ready to pounce on his prey. He was waiting. Listening. Watching. It was only a matter of time, he determined, before Julie did or said something to give herself away.

She'd never followed the rules before. Why should now be any different? As he'd warned Ellie earlier, Julie would play down and dirty.

To Buck's surprise, Julie said nothing at all. She smiled a few times when Tyler was especially animated, and she never took her eyes off the boy, but she didn't speak, not even to ask him a question. From time to time she'd put her fork in her mouth, but Buck could tell her mind wasn't on the meal before her any more than his was.

As soon as he'd scarfed down his food, Tyler asked to be excused from the table and bounded out of his chair to go spend time with his colt. As soon as Tyler was gone, Buck pushed away from the table and stood, nodding to the ladies. "I'm going to go for a walk," he said.

He didn't even make it out the back door before Julie was hot on his heels.

"Buck, wait," she called frantically.

Buck froze for a moment, allowing Julie to catch up before adjusting his long stride to match her shorter one, his boots soft against the well-worn trail. He shoved his hands into the pockets of his jeans jacket and glanced furtively at the woman he'd once called his wife.

She was flushed from the walk, and Buck slowed his pace even more. He tempered his urge to run, to bolt for the stable. He knew he could easily outpace her and have a horse saddled before she even made it to the stable. It took all his self-control to keep from doing just that.

"I can't do this," she said, pulling in a deep breath and clenching her hands in front of her.

"What?" Buck whirled on her in surprise. "What do you mean, you can't do this? You already have."

"I know," she admitted with a short nod. "I realize now that I've tipped the balance. I was thinking only of myself when I came here. I didn't realize how it was going to affect you."

"How do you mean?"

She shook her head before feinting out of the question. "You've done a fine job raising Tyler."

"No thanks to you," Buck growled before he could think better of it. "It wasn't easy. I struggled for many years to get where I am now. And Tyler has really come out of his shell now that Ellie is here to give him a mother's guidance."

"Something I never did," Julie admitted. "I was never good mother material, never mind being a decent wife. And that's another thing."

Buck just stared at her, wondering where she was going with all this.

"Your relationship with Ellie," Julie stated.

Buck didn't know what to say, so he remained silent, but he wasn't about to deny the relationship he'd built with Ellie if Julie pushed him on the subject.

"I've seen the way you look at her."

"And…?"

"And I'm happy for you. I really am. Ellie obviously loves you—and Tyler. I'm glad to see you've really moved on with your life, and I know Ellie makes you happy."

Buck shook his head, his eyes narrowing on Julie. "Why do I feel there's more to this? You suddenly having the overwhelming compulsion to see the son you abandoned ten years ago? Tell me the truth, Julie." He placed a foot on the corral fence and leaned his elbows into the hard strength of the wood, choosing to stare out into the range rather than to look straight at his ex.

"Look, I don't know how to say this, or how you will take it, so I'm just going to be blunt," Julie said suddenly with a rush of air. "Things went downhill the moment I left you, Buck. I was really young and immature and stupid. I did so many, many things I regret."

Buck didn't answer, though privately he agreed with her assessment.

"I got into a lot of trouble before God pulled me out of the mire," she continued when Buck didn't speak. "I have asked His forgiveness, but I came here to ask for yours, on behalf of both you and Tyler."

Buck felt as if he were turned to stone. He wasn't ready to forgive Julie. He wasn't sure he ever would be. But to his surprise, the rush of anger and disappointment he expected to experience never came.

"I'm about to be married to a wonderful Christian man—a minister," Julie continued. "If I can help it, I don't want to go into this marriage with such a large burden on my soul. Can you understand that?"

Buck scrubbed his palms across his eyes against the terrible headache forming in his temples. He thought his head might pop from too much information, too quickly.

"I'll leave first thing in the morning," she continued softly when Buck didn't say anything. "I promise I won't try to talk to Tyler, though I'll admit it gave me great joy to sit through dinner with him. He was so animated. And happy."

"I don't think you should go, leaving things as they are." He hadn't thought about what he was saying. The words just appeared out of nowhere, jumping out of his mouth several seconds before he realized it was the right thing for him to say.

"Are you sure?" she probed.

"No."

Julie laughed shakily at Buck's clipped answer.

Buck's gaze drifted toward Julie. He suddenly realized he wasn't the only one who'd changed over the years. Julie had learned from her experiences. From what she'd told him, she'd had her fair share of trials.

If she'd really changed, was it fair of him to deny her the right to see her son?

Maybe more to the point, was it fair to Tyler to keep this knowledge a secret? Now that Julie had found Christ and was taking full responsibility for her past sins, would Tyler want to get to know her as his biological mother?

He didn't meet Julie's gaze until she touched his arm. He turned to her then, and she stared at him as if she were trying to read the truth in his eyes.

He wished her luck. He didn't know what the truth was anymore. She certainly wasn't going to find anything searching his gaze.

"What made you change your mind?" she asked softly, still touching his elbow.

"I'm not entirely sure I have," Buck answered curtly,

stemming the instinctive urge to brush her hand off his arm. "I don't want Tyler to be hurt. I've spent my whole life protecting him, and I'm not going to stop now."

Julie's gaze didn't waver as she nodded.

"That said, you *are* his biological mother, and that's a fact. A boy should know his mother."

"Even if there's another woman ready to step into that role?" Julie queried softly.

His heart clenched. Would Ellie even want to become his wife and be a mother to Tyler? With everything being what it was, he truly didn't know.

Despite her best intentions not to give in to the emotions swirling inside her, Ellie broke down and had herself a good cry the moment Buck and Julie were out the door. It didn't take but a few minutes to cry herself out, after which she splashed cool water on her face. She examined herself in the mirror to make sure there were no telltale signs of her weakness, then began to clear the table.

She had just finished washing the dishes in the sink and was running a towel over the last of the plates when Buck and Julie came in through the back door. Determined to be the sanctuary Buck needed, a good friend and not a freaked-out girlfriend—or whatever she was—Ellie squared her shoulders and turned to face Buck and his ex.

Buck's hands were shoved in the pockets of his jeans, and he looked like he might jump right out of his skin. He was literally shaking from the effort to keep himself steady, and Ellie felt strangely comforted by the fact that she wasn't the only one suffering from

Julie's sudden appearance, though that was hardly fair. It wasn't his fault Julie was here. Ellie silently renewed the promise to herself and God that she would stand by Buck no matter what happened between them now.

Julie's expression was oddly peaceful, though signs of her recent distress were still clearly visible. Ellie wondered what had transpired, but she didn't want to prod. She couldn't help but be curious, though, even if she wouldn't so much as consider expressing her interest out loud. The differences in Buck's and Julie's expressions were enough to let Ellie know something had changed while they'd been outside.

Ellie wanted to grasp Buck's hand and give it a reassuring squeeze, but felt uncomfortable showing her affection for him with Julie in the room. In the end she simply tossed the dish towel over her shoulder, folded her arms in front of her and waited for someone to speak.

Buck took a step toward Ellie, cocking his head so their eyes met. He smiled, but it was shaky at best. Ellie just stared, her eyes widening under the strength of his gaze. It seemed like hours passed between them, though Ellie knew it must have been no longer than a few seconds.

"Hmm," Buck murmured and then took her chin in his hand, tipping her face up. Arching one eyebrow, he took the index finger of his other hand and attempted to pull one corner of Ellie's mouth into a smile. She tried to accommodate him, but it must have looked more like a grimace than a smile, if the frown that suddenly wrinkled Buck's brow was anything to go by.

"Can we sit down, please?" Julie prompted, gesturing to the kitchen table. "We need to talk."

"I'll just be in the living room, cleaning up," Ellie immediately replied, thinking Buck and Julie must still need their privacy to work things out.

"No, no!" Julie exclaimed. "Buck and I definitely need you here with us."

Ellie cringed inwardly at the words *Buck and I.* She hated that she was jealous of the woman who'd left Buck and Tyler years ago, but there it was, staring her right in the face. It gave Ellie a new appreciation for the words *green monster.* Buck had once cared enough about Julie to marry her and have a child with her. And though Ellie considered the years spent putting elbow-grease into her ministry worthwhile, the fact was, Buck had at some point moved on with his life and had a family to show for it, whereas Ellie was alone. And she had never felt more so than at this moment.

Ellie knew it would take a good deal of prayer to straighten out her heart on this issue, but this was obviously not the time. Buck had already shown Julie to a seat and was now standing behind an empty chair, gesturing for Ellie to sit.

Ellie gritted her teeth and sat. Whatever problems she was facing would have to wait. There was a difference between *feeling* and *acting.* She would force herself to respond with compassion and hope her feelings would catch up later.

It wasn't easy.

Buck took the hard-backed chair next to Ellie and turned it around, straddling the chair and leaning his elbows on the back as he usually did. His fists were still clenched, and there was a dent in his brow, which Ellie thought must have been caused by the stress he was feeling. She tamped back the urge to wipe the anxiety off his forehead with the tips of her fingers.

Buck and Julie were staring at each other. Ellie suspected they were trying to decide who, between the two of them, would speak first.

It didn't look like either one of them was in a big hurry to talk at all, which just frustrated Ellie all the more. She could feel Buck's tension, like electrical static in the air, though, strangely enough, Julie didn't appear to be suffering from much of the same anxiety. Her eyes looked sad, not angry, and her lips twitched in and out of a smile.

"So," Ellie began when Buck and Julie continued their uncomfortable silence, "have you decided what you want to do here?"

"Yes," Buck said.

"No," said Julie simultaneously.

Ellie chuckled dryly. At least she had got them talking. "Okay. Which is it?"

"Yes."

"No." Again overlapping.

Ellie slid a look at Buck before addressing Julie. "Maybe I should leave you two alone a bit longer," she said hesitantly, trying to keep an open mind and a blank expression, not entirely successful with either one.

"No." This time they agreed at least.

Ellie felt like sprinting out of the room. Instead she laid her palms flat down on the cool walnut table. A direct approach was obviously called for here, or they would get nowhere. "What have you decided about Tyler?"

"Buck thinks I should tell Tyler who I am, but I don't think that would be the best idea." Julie's words came quickly and nearly on top of each other in her haste to speak. She finished her statement and swept in a deep, audible breath.

Ellie was certain her jaw dropped. Her eyes definitely widened in surprise. She had expected just the opposite from what Julie was saying. A mere hour ago Buck had wanted Julie to leave posthaste, and it had been Julie who had insisted on staying.

What had changed?

"Wasn't that your whole reason for coming here?" The question sounded a little defensive even to her own ears, but Ellie couldn't help it.

Not where Tyler was concerned.

"Julie's reason for coming here isn't as convoluted as I first thought it was," Buck murmured, his smile fading as he looked back at his ex. He shrugged grudgingly. "She's not here on a whim, just to make our lives miserable and spring herself on Tyler."

"Yeah, I got that," Ellie murmured, and then she turned her attention to Julie as the other woman began to tell the story—the *whole* story—of why she'd come here. *Now.*

When Julie was finished talking, Ellie let out the breath she'd been holding. She had to admit she was surprised by what she had learned.

Julie was a *Christian?* Did that change everything, or not? Ellie wasn't sure.

"That's why I think she should tell Tyler the truth," Buck explained, his voice low and gravelly. "There's been more than enough pain and betrayal in our lives already. It might help Tyler to learn the truth about his birth mother. I thought maybe it would help him resolve his anger issues."

"Only if you agree that's what is best, too, Ellie," Julie speedily added as a postscript.

"What does this have to do with me?" Ellie asked Julie, shaking her head in denial. "This decision has to be exclusively between you and Buck."

"I told her you didn't want to get in the middle of this," Buck rumbled.

Ellie's gaze flashed back to Buck. She wondered if Julie could see the pain etched in Buck's features, as Ellie could. How close had Buck and Julie once been? And was the bond of having a child together so easily broken?

"Perhaps I was wrong about that," Ellie admitted softly. "I might have been trying to take the easy way out. I want to be there for you, Buck, and for Tyler, too."

"You do?" Buck swept in a deep breath, and his expression immediately brightened up at the first sound of her heartfelt declaration.

"Of course I do," Ellie assured him. "I, er, care for you, you knucklehead." Ellie was still uncomfortable expressing the deepest emotions of her heart in front of Buck's ex, but she didn't see any way around it now.

And Buck needed to hear it.

"But you just said you didn't think this situation— Julie coming clean to the *whole* family—had anything to do with you," he pointed out. It almost sounded like an accusation.

"That's right. I did. Because what you and Julie

decide to do shouldn't have anything to do with me," Ellie explained, her tone slightly defensive.

"But it does, don't you see?" Julie finally shifted her gaze from the table to Ellie. "This has everything to do with you."

"You want my opinion?" Ellie asked, confused.

"We want more than your opinion, Ellie," Buck added. "Julie and I—and most especially Tyler—we all need your support, no matter what decision we come to tonight. You offered, and I'm holding you to it. We need you."

"Don't you think Tyler already thinks of you as a mother?" Julie queried.

Ellie hadn't really thought about that. It had been so natural to protect and nurture Tyler—almost as if he were her own son, and not Julie's. Maybe because Julie had been out of the picture. She had abandoned her family.

Until now.

Ellie leveled her gaze on Julie, who looked as if she wanted to turn away, though she didn't.

"I agree with Buck," Ellie said so softly she wasn't sure anyone had heard.

"You do?" Buck sounded surprised.

"Based on everything you've told me, Julie, it doesn't seem right to keep this a secret any longer," Ellie added.

"We should hold off on telling him until tomorrow, though," Buck stated firmly. "Tyler had the best birthday party ever today. His *only* birthday party ever. We don't know which way this is going to go. Let's not ruin his day."

"I say we sleep on it," Ellie suggested. "Pray about it. Morning will be soon enough to make a final decision."

Buck flashed her a relieved grin. "See?" he told Julie. "I told you Ellie was special."

Ellie blushed, wondering how *special* she would feel tomorrow, when Tyler found out who Julie really was. Would the boy still want Ellie in his life? Or would Julie's presence ruin the best two things that had ever happened to her?

Chapter Twelve

Morning came too early for Buck, who had spent the better part of the night pacing back and forth across the small confines of his room like a caged animal. He'd prayed harder than he'd ever prayed in his life. He'd searched the scriptures, reading the psalms to find a small degree of comfort.

But it wasn't enough.

Or at least, it didn't feel like enough. Buck knew better than to attach too much significance to his feelings, but he couldn't shake the sensation that he was carrying around a tremendously heavy burden on his shoulders.

Truth be told, Buck was out-and-out terrified of what the morning would bring. Despite his brave face to Ellie, he wasn't one hundred percent convinced they were doing the right thing. What if everything went south? What if the last person Tyler wanted to meet in his life was his biological mother?

What if Buck was wrong? And how could he live with himself if he was?

Buck found both women already in the kitchen, seated across from each other and silently sipping their mugs of coffee. Each of the women was studiously avoiding the other, but Ellie looked up at him when he entered the room.

Ellie had obviously not slept any better than Buck, judging from the black circles under her eyes. Julie, while not looking well rested exactly, at least looked determined, her lips pinching together after every sip of coffee.

Buck poured a cup of steaming coffee for himself and sat down next to Ellie.

"So?" he asked after taking a long pull of the hot liquid. The coffee burned his throat, but it was a welcome distraction from the tension lacing the air.

Ellie gazed at him questioningly. Julie took another sip of coffee.

"Are we still on the same page?" he asked when neither woman spoke.

"I think so," Ellie murmured, nodding her head. "If Julie is willing to make amends, I don't see how it's fair to let her walk away without Tyler knowing the truth."

Buck nodded.

"Fair to Tyler, that is," Ellie added quickly. "The boy is old enough to make his own decisions on whether or not he wants to pursue any kind of relationship with Julie. We need to be honest with him."

Buck's gaze widened on Ellie. All through the night he had been praying for answers, praying that his son would not be hurt by their decision to come clean. While he'd given great consideration to how

Tyler would react, he hadn't realized he had done his son a disservice, had underestimated the boy—the young man.

Tyler *did* deserve to know the truth, Buck recognized belatedly. He wasn't a small child anymore. Hadn't Tyler shown Buck in so many ways just how grown up he was?

Julie's fingers were gripping the mug so tightly, Buck marveled that it didn't break in her hands. Her expression was equally apprehensive.

Buck exhaled sharply. "So, how are we going to go about this?" he asked quietly.

"Go about what?" came an all-too-familiar voice from the doorway.

Buck froze, his coffee cup midway to his mouth. Ellie straightened. Julie slumped.

"What's going on?" Tyler asked, his gaze sliding from face to face. The boy rubbed his palms over his eyes in a sleepy fashion usually reserved for toddlers, the unconscious gesture bringing with it a boulder-size lump to Buck's throat.

However the three adults had envisioned everything going down, this most certainly wasn't it. Yet his son was clearly intrigued by the fact that nobody was speaking. Ellie, at least, should be bubbling over right about now, even if Buck was his usual silent self.

And then there was Julie….

Buck slid his gaze from Tyler to Julie, who was staring at the boy with wide eyes and a slack jaw, which worked up and down as if she meant to speak, though no sound crossed her lips. Buck's fingers started a rhythmic staccato against the cool hardness of the walnut table, in tune with the persistent thrumming of his angst-ridden heart.

"I...I..." Julie said at last, but even the single syllable sounded garbled to Buck's ears.

Buck panicked. His fingers continued their droning, but he hardly noticed through the haze of emotion hanging over him. The adults in question needed to *plan* a time and place to tell the boy the truth, not just spring it on him because he had entered the kitchen at the wrong moment.

Buck tried to get Julie's attention but failed. Her gaze never left Tyler.

Ellie's hand was somehow in Buck's. She squeezed hard, silencing the nervous movement of his wayward fingers. The tension-laden air now felt to Buck as if it were full of razor-sharp shards of glass. He tried to breathe normally but couldn't, as the air painfully stuck in his lungs.

Julie shook herself, as if coming out of a trance. She looked to Buck hesitantly. "Should I..." She stopped herself and started over again. "Should we tell him?"

Tyler frowned straight at Buck, clearly blaming him for any secrets being kept. Buck would have cringed if he could move, but he was still frozen to the spot.

After a moment Tyler huffed in exasperation and turned his gaze upon Ellie. "Tell me what?"

Ellie coughed, clearing her throat. "Your dad and Julie have something they want to say to you."

Tyler's eyes flitted back to Buck again, his gaze narrowing in suspicion. "Dad and *Julie?*"

Buck sighed loudly. This wasn't going the way he thought it would, not that he'd actually come up with a likely scenario for telling Tyler anything without hurting the boy's feelings. *But still,* he thought, a war waging inside his heart.

And now it couldn't be helped.

"Julie didn't come here for the therapy ranch," Buck explained, wondering if his voice sounded as strained to his son as it did to his own ears. "She came here for you."

The sudden brightness, followed by a flash of pain, in Tyler's eyes was enough for Buck to know the boy had more than an inkling of what Buck was talking about, what he could not bring himself to say aloud.

"And?" Tyler asked through clenched teeth.

And? Tyler stared Buck straight in the eyes, daring him with both his gaze and his posture. He was going to make Buck say the words out loud.

This time Buck did cringe, visibly. He looked to Julie for help. This was her problem, after all. Buck hadn't invited her here, nor did he particularly want what was happening, even if last evening he'd been encouraging Julie toward just this outcome.

"And, uh…" Buck stalled, trying to swim through the murk of his confusion. If only he wasn't so suddenly set on doing what was right, he might lie through his teeth and make it all go away.

Yet despite the noise in his head, Buck knew he needed to do what *God* would have him do, no matter what—not take what would clearly be the easiest way out, for a change. Maybe for the first time in his life.

"We didn't want you to find out this way," Ellie said in a soothing tone. "But now that you're here, you need to know the truth."

Tyler already had his arms crossed, and now he

took a step backward. The boy's scowl deepened, if that were possible, Buck thought.

"Julie is your...uh..." Buck tried his best, but he couldn't choke out the word. He turned his gaze to Ellie, pleading silently for her to finish his sentence.

"Julie is your birth mother." Ellie's words came out in a rush of air, one on top of the other.

Time seemed to stand still as Tyler absorbed the news. Suspecting was one thing. Hearing it out loud was another thing entirely. Tyler shook his head slowly from side to side, still in slow motion; at least it felt that way to Buck.

"No." The young man's hands came abruptly down to his sides in fists. The single word was quiet, the protest uttered through Tyler's clenched teeth. The boy slid his gaze from face to face, his eyes narrowing until they rested on Buck.

"No!" Tyler exclaimed, louder this time. He smashed his now-open palm into the back of an empty chair, which slapped violently against the table before it teetered and fell to the floor with a loud clatter.

Howling in fury, Tyler swung on his heels and dashed through the back door and out of the house. Buck watched him go, too dazed to do anything but look. His heart was breaking into a million tiny pieces.

"Well," Ellie said on a sigh, "that's about what we expected, isn't it?"

Ellie squeezed Buck's hand again, mumbling compassionate reassurances under her breath.

"Should I... Should I go after him?" Julie stammered hesitantly, tucking her short blond hair behind her ears.

Buck shook his head and then clamped a thumb and

forefinger over his temple, where a sudden headache had developed like a spring thunderstorm. He took a ragged breath. "No," he said, groaning at the stabbing pain in his head. "I'll do it."

Ellie squeezed his hand again, and he lost himself for a moment in her compassionate gaze.

"Everything is going to be fine," she reassured him, her voice low and even, though her hand was shaking.

Buck nodded, though he wasn't the least bit sure *everything* would ever be fine again. He stood and jammed his cowboy hat on his head, pulling the front tip low over his brow, shading his gaze from the ladies.

Julie might not notice any change in his expression, but Ellie had a gift that way. She was sure to see the telltale moisture in his eyes, a weakness that he most desperately wanted to hide.

"Maybe you should give him a few minutes to cool down," Ellie suggested kindly.

Buck nodded once again, short and clipped. "I'll take my time getting down there. I need to pray about what I'm going to say, anyway."

"You know where he's going?" Julie asked, her eyebrows arching in surprise.

He chuckled, but it was a dead sound. He moved his gaze back to Ellie, who was nodding.

"I have a pretty good idea where to find him," Buck informed his ex-wife.

"Are you sure I shouldn't go with you?" Julie queried. "This is all my fault."

"No," Buck replied testily, and then he inhaled sharply. "I mean, I think it's better if I talk to Tyler on my own first—to try to get him to see reason, you know?"

Julie cringed. Ellie reached across the table to pat Julie's shoulder, a comforting gesture Buck wished was meant for him and not his ex-wife. That Ellie was here at all was a show of just how deep her faith ran and how strong her character was.

Buck loved Ellie more in that moment than he thought possible. He silently thanked God again for his second chance with Ellie and prayed the present circumstances hadn't ruined everything. He tipped his hat to the ladies and exited through the back door, the way Tyler had gone.

Buck *did* know where Tyler had gone—at least he thought he did. His mind flashed back to the first day here on Ellie's ranch, the day Tyler had helped Ellie deliver the little colt that now belonged to him. It only made sense, didn't it, for Tyler to find solace in the company of the horses he loved so much?

Still, Buck took his time, scuffling slowly down the hill and toward the stable, in no hurry to confront his angry son, even though he knew it needed to be done, and he was the one to do it. His own heart was still rocking from Julie's betrayal, though the years—and his new relationship with Ellie—eased that pain somewhat.

But for Tyler, this was all new.

His son had been too young to really remember his mother. It pained Buck to speak of Julie, so he hadn't, brushing off young Tyler's questions about his mother until the boy no longer asked.

Buck scoffed and shook his head, though he was walking alone, with no one to see. Had he inadvertently made things worse for his son?

As Buck ambled down the hill, he noticed dust

rising from the corral. He had thought Tyler would be hiding in the stable, so he was surprised to see the boy out in plain sight, putting one of the horses through training motions.

Buck approached the corral quietly, leaning on the railing to watch his son in action. Tyler, his camel-colored hat as low over his brow as Buck's own, didn't seem to notice his advancement; or if he did, he didn't let on that he knew Buck was there.

For a moment Buck let him be. Tyler would speak when he was ready.

Buck couldn't help but smile as he watched his son work. Tyler had a rope halter over Sophie, the new colt's dam. The boy was leading her around the stall, slowly letting out the lead as he turned, until the mare was trotting around the outer rim of the corral.

At her heels was Jet, gamboling around the corral, trying to keep up with his mother.

Pride welled up in Buck's chest. Tyler had obviously been paying attention to Buck's work with horses over the years. The boy instinctively knew that the first step in training the colt was to have him mimic his mother's paces. Before Buck knew it, Tyler would be leading Jet around with a halter of his own.

Buck nodded enthusiastically as Tyler turned his direction. The boy ignored him and quickly turned his back on Buck, but Buck could hear Tyler encouraging the mare—and the colt—with soft, gentle nonsense words.

Dust flew as Tyler nudged the mare into a canter. The colt, confused by the sudden change of velocity and unable to keep up with his mother, bucked and pawed at the ground in the center of the corral. Buck chuckled at the little horse's antics, especially when Jet began nosing his muzzle into Tyler's side, under his arm, near the chest pocket of his flannel shirt, where, Buck guessed, Tyler had stashed some sugar cubes.

At the sound of Buck's laugh, Tyler froze, still turned away from his father. The mare continued galloping around the corral, but Tyler no longer held her in check with the lead, which was dangling loosely. His hands were once again curled into fists, and Buck thought he saw his son's shoulders quivering.

Crying?

Buck couldn't blame Tyler for his tears, but it sure broke his heart to see his son in so much pain. Buck had never been one to cotton to the old "Real men don't cry" adage, which his own father had pushed on him, even if he himself had serious issues with expressing emotion.

"Son," he called over the clamor of the horses' hooves. "Tyler. Are you okay?"

Now Buck could definitely see Tyler's shoulders shaking, and he wondered what he could possibly say to ease the situation, to rub away the hurt.

Were there words?

Buck had never been good speaking his feelings aloud, and this was no exception. Clearly this was not the best approach, but he couldn't think of a single other thing to say that wouldn't make things worse.

"Tyler?" he called again.

"Just. Leave. Me. Alone," Tyler hissed, without turning around to face his father.

Buck shook his head, only belatedly aware that Tyler couldn't see the movement.

"No, son," he said at last and then cleared his throat against his smoky voice. "I'm sorry. I can't do that."

Tyler turned then, swiveling so quickly Buck barely saw him move. Buck's gaze was fixed on his son's face. He had expected pain. Grief. Sadness.

He was taken aback, for all he saw in his son's narrowed, piercing gaze was anger.

Ellie had no idea what to do with Julie while Buck was talking to Tyler. She was so uncomfortable, she almost wanted to jump out of her own skin. She could think of nothing to say to Buck's ex-wife—at least nothing kind.

Besides, her mind was on Tyler. It was heart-wrenching enough just to have been in the room with Buck, especially when Tyler had come in. What must the boy have thought, having such colossal information just flung at him out of the blue?

It certainly wasn't the way Ellie would have done it, though, truth be told, she couldn't think of a single way that *would* have saved Tyler the angst he was now facing.

It was obvious Julie was pondering the same thing. Her mouth was twisted, and she was clasping her hands in a repetitive, though not rhythmic, motion. Julie's blond hair had fallen into her face, but she didn't brush it back.

Not wanting to sit and stare at the woman, Ellie got up and reached for the coffeepot, refilling both their mugs with the steaming liquid. At least that gave her something to do with her hands, however small. She contemplated cleaning the oven—from top to bottom. *Now.*

She would have laughed at the picture that made if the circumstances weren't so serious. Ellie thought she should say something to Julie, but she didn't know what.

"The last thing I meant to do was to hurt him," Julie said, still wringing her hands.

"Tyler?" Ellie asked.

Julie lifted her gaze. "Tyler," she agreed, her lips still pinched. "And Buck."

Ellie blinked a couple of times. In her head she knew Julie wasn't being possessive—she was just stating facts. But Ellie's heart didn't want to agree.

"How long do you think they'll be?" Julie asked, furtively glancing at her watch.

Ellie shrugged, not bothering to look at the clock. "I don't know. A while, probably. I wouldn't be surprised if Buck has to chase Tyler all around the ranch to get him to listen. Tyler's a bit stubborn that way."

"Just like his father," Julie noted. She chuckled, but it was a dry sound.

Ellie nodded. Yes, Tyler was like Buck, in more ways than she could count. What would happen if they couldn't work through this situation? She might lose them both.

"And his age," Ellie said belatedly. "Teenagers definitely have minds of their own."

"Thirteen," Julie murmured. "The years seem like they are getting shorter and shorter."

"They do, don't they?" Ellie said contemplatively. "I remember when I was a teenager. It seemed to me as if a year would last forever."

At least until Buck had left.

The first few years, Ellie remembered with a dull stab of pain in the general area of her heart, had

stretched on interminably. She had thrown herself wholeheartedly into her college studies and then, with God's grace, she'd found her therapy ranch ministry.

And now she had found Buck again and had fallen in love with both him and his son.

Julie pushed her hair back and looked at her watch again, impatience lining her brow.

"This is going to take some time," Ellie reiterated, not so much to remind Julie as to soothe her own fears. "I'd better brew another pot of coffee."

Chapter Thirteen

Anger.

Tyler was staring at Buck with pure, unadulterated rage. Buck would go so far as to say there was downright *hatred* in his son's expression. Buck assumed that particular emotion was aimed at him as much as at Julie.

And who could blame the kid?

Buck was angry at himself. While it was true that Julie had deserted him and Tyler, Buck had been the one to carry a grudge all these years. A grudge that ultimately had hurt his son.

He couldn't change the past. But he could do his best to make amends now.

"I'm sorry you had to meet her this way," Buck said, reaching over the fence to grab the mare's lead away from Tyler and slow the horse to a skittering halt. "I didn't mean for you to meet her this way."

"Whatever." Tyler sniffed and pulled his hat even lower over his eyes.

They were back to that, then.

"No, not *whatever,* son. You can't just walk away from this. *We* can't walk away from this."

"Why not?" Tyler challenged.

Buck kicked himself over the fence in one leap and then strode to Tyler's side, wrapping his arms around the boy before he could scamper away. He held on tightly until Tyler stopped squirming in his grip.

"Julie is your mother, champ."

"That woman is *not* my mother." Tyler had frozen rock solid in Buck's grip.

"Yes, she is," Buck maintained in a monotone voice. "Well, your biological mother, anyway."

Tyler jerked his shoulder, breaking Buck's grip. The boy beelined for the stable. Buck regained the mare's halter and led her and the foal into the stable at a slower pace, purposefully giving Tyler a moment to compose himself.

As Buck expected, Tyler was slumped in the hay in a back corner of the birthing stall, his arms locked around his knees, his hands gripping his wrists. His head was down, hiding his expression, but Buck could hear that Tyler was crying.

It broke his heart. Again.

"I'm sorry, son," Buck said on a sigh. Absently he removed the halter from the mare and rubbed her down.

"You're *sorry?*" Tyler accused.

"I have a lot of regrets in my life," Buck admitted quietly, crouching before Tyler.

"Like me?" Tyler mumbled under his breath, so softly Buck barely heard the words.

"No!" Buck exclaimed. He lifted his hands to cup Tyler's face, forcing the boy to look at him. "Never."

He could tell Tyler didn't believe him, as pain over-shadowed the anger in the boy's shiny blue eyes. Tyler's pain echoed in the deepest recesses of Buck's heart, like his insides were being cut out with a dull knife.

"Never," Buck repeated, stronger this time. "Never, ever. Not one single day, Tyler. There's nothing in my life more important to me than you."

Tyler blinked in rapid succession, but tears still slipped through his eyelids. Buck brushed the wetness away with the pads of his thumbs.

"What I regret," Buck continued, "is not telling you the whole truth about your mother. I thought it would be easier for you if I let you think whatever you wanted about her. Now I see I gave you ample space to create your own reality, one that was even worse than the truth."

"That my *mother* left because of me," Tyler hissed, his tone bitter.

"No!" Buck exclaimed again. "None of this was your fault. You have to believe that."

Tyler didn't answer.

Buck took a deep breath and plunged forward. "You should know that Julie came here with the intention of making amends—to tell you she's sorry for not being there for you when you were growing up."

"Why *now?*"

"She became a Christian, Tyler," Buck explained quietly. "She didn't want to go through the rest of her life without asking for your forgiveness."

"It's not *fair*," Tyler insisted. "I hate her. Julie has ruined *everything!*"

Buck cringed. It wouldn't do for Tyler to carry his hatred like a beacon around his neck. Buck should know. Wasn't that exactly what *he* had done, not only in the past ten years with Julie, but before that, with the quarrel with his own mother? And he had blamed God, he realized, for everything that went wrong in his life.

"It won't do you any good," he said aloud, his voice raspy. "Hating your mother will only make you miserable."

"It won't do any *good?*" Tyler echoed, his voice becoming more high-pitched by the moment. He brushed Buck's hands away. "You won't even *try,* Dad. How fair is that?"

Buck's brow creased as he considered his son's words. "I'm not sure I follow you."

Tyler glared at Buck and then rolled his eyes, as if his father was the stupidest man alive. Maybe he was.

"Make her go away," Tyler snapped.

Buck sat down by his son, groaning as he leaned his back against the wall. He stared at Tyler for a good minute without speaking.

"Okay, I will," he said slowly, thoughtfully. "If that's what you really want."

"You will?" Tyler asked, relief flooding into his shaky voice. He actually sounded hopeful, which immediately played on Buck's heartstrings. "Really?"

Buck nodded solemnly. "Of course I will. But I think you should think about this first. Your mother…"

Tyler leveled him with a glare.

"*Julie* has come a long way to see you. She lives in California now."

"So?"

"She might not deserve our forgiveness," Buck admitted, patting his son's arm. "But look at it from another perspective. Jesus saved us—*forgave* us—knowing every misdeed in our past and all the wrong things we have yet to do. If God is willing to do that for us, can we do any less?"

Tyler laughed bitterly. "Did Ellie tell you that? Since when did you become a preacher?"

One corner of Buck's lips rose just slightly. It was the first time since Julie had arrived at the door that he really felt any relief from the black storm clouds that seemed to have descended on him. "I'm no preacher."

Tyler scoffed. "No kidding."

"But I remember the Lord's Prayer. You know, 'forgive us our trespasses, as we forgive those who trespass against us'? Sound familiar?"

Tyler shrugged. "I guess."

"Look, son. I know I'm not the best role model. I was mad at your grandma for a long time for something she did—for so long I practically forgot why I was mad at her in the first place. For the longest time I refused to speak to her, though she tried over and over to contact me."

Tyler sniffed and wiped his eyes, his attention clearly focused on Buck.

"Then what happened?"

"When your mother...when *Julie* left, I felt betrayed all over again. This time it was Julie who wouldn't talk to me. I guess I eventually got it through my thick skull that I had done the same thing to my mother—your grandmother."

"Yeah," Tyler agreed. "At least you worked it out with Grandma."

Buck nodded. "I did. But it wasn't easy. And if I

hadn't been so bullheaded, I wouldn't have wasted so many years hating when there's so much room to love."

"But, Dad, I—I don't love Julie," Tyler stammered and then cleared his throat.

"No one expects you to," Buck assured him. "I certainly don't, and Julie doesn't love me, either."

"What, then?"

"She just wants to talk to you. Apologize for her past behavior. Get to know the great son she has, you know, before you're all grown up on us."

"What about Ellie?" Tyler challenged.

"What about Ellie?" Buck repeated softly, the very mention of her name making his heart start skittering like the newborn colt.

Tyler groaned. "Aw, Dad, don't make me say it."

"I wouldn't if I had the slightest idea what you were talking about," Buck said with a laugh.

"*You* and Ellie."

A new understanding washed over Buck. So that was what this was all about.

"You don't think Julie being here is going to affect the way I feel about Ellie or how she feels about you, do you?" Buck asked, honestly perplexed.

Tyler shrugged. "Maybe."

"Not in this lifetime," Buck assured his son. He stood to his feet, brushed the hay off his jeans and offered a hand to Tyler. "You think I'm going to let a woman like Ellie off the hook?"

"You did once," Tyler reminded him, accepting the hand Buck offered and pulling himself to his feet, then, following his father's lead, brushing the hay off his jeans.

"And I learned from that experience. I may be slow, but I'm not stupid."

Tyler laughed. "So what are we going to do, then?"

Surprisingly, Buck knew the answer to that question. It was all about trust, wasn't it? Ellie needed to know he wasn't going to walk out on her again, that he was here for good this time.

And he knew just how to do that. He grinned at Tyler. "I have an idea."

Would this day never end?

Would this tension ever slacken?

Would this pain never cease?

Ellie glanced at the clock over the sink for the tenth time in as many minutes. At first, it had only been Julie staring at her watch.

Now they were both clock watching, waiting with a mixture of anticipation and trepidation so thick in the air, Ellie thought she could almost slice it. It was definitely difficult for her to breathe. Getting air to her lungs was no longer an involuntary act. She had to coach herself.

In, two, three. Out, two, three.

A movement at the doorway had Ellie on her feet even before Julie. Both women stared at the door as Tyler entered, followed by Buck, who swept his hat off his head and sighed loudly, his expression giving nothing away.

Tyler mimicked his father's movement, but the young man didn't have the same ability to mask his features that his father did. Ellie recognized the joy streaming from Tyler's gaze before the excited grin on his face even registered with her.

Her heart sank, and a weight grew painfully heavy on her shoulders.

What did it mean, that joy in Tyler's eyes? Ellie wondered. That he was glad to meet his birth mother? Ellie would have thought Buck would have had to drag the boy kicking and screaming back to the house.

Apparently Tyler was much more resilient than Ellie had previously determined him to be. She had hoped for the best, but now that it was here, she wasn't sure that was really what she wanted. She had basked in the new love she'd found with Buck and Tyler. Now she would have to learn to share that love. It might be the right thing to do, but it wasn't easy. She slid her glance to Julie, who was flushed and beaming at her son.

Ellie moved her gaze to Buck, who pulled up one side of his mouth in what could have passed for a half smile, or maybe a grimace. His eyes flittered from hers, but not before she'd read his expression.

Guilty as charged.

"Tyler," Buck pressed when the young man didn't immediately speak.

Ellie purposefully avoided looking at Tyler again, afraid she might burst into tears. Never in a million years would she have expected things to go this way.

Tyler stepped forward into Ellie's view. Despite her reticence, Ellie found herself drawn to the scene of the young man approaching the mother he barely remembered. His intent, Ellie surmised, was clear enough from the grin on his face.

Obviously Julie thought so, too, for she stepped closer to the boy and held out her hand to him. His expression turning suddenly serious, Tyler took Julie's proffered hand and shook it solemnly, looking every inch the young man he was.

"It's nice to meet you, ma'am," he said and then glanced at Ellie, as if requesting confirmation for his actions.

Ellie thought her heart might rip in two, but she forced herself to smile and nod at the boy, hoping her expression was encouraging and did not reveal her true state of mind.

"I'm glad to…" Julie paused and tripped over her words. "To meet you, too, Tyler."

"Yeah," the boy agreed, but his smile was wavering.

Buck stepped forward and laid a reassuring hand on Tyler's shoulder.

"Tyler has agreed to speak with you," he said, addressing Julie.

"I'm so glad," Julie gushed.

"However," Buck continued. Ellie noted how he squeezed his son's shoulder. "I know you've been waiting a long time, but I hope you will be willing to postpone this, er, reunion, until later. Tyler and I have something important to discuss with Ellie."

"Of course," said Julie, standing. "I have some phone calls to make."

Julie's exit was more graceful than Ellie imagined her own would have been.

She wanted to dash out of the house as quickly as she could. She didn't have any desire whatsoever to hear what Tyler and Buck had to say. Given the way things were going, it could only be bad news for her.

She couldn't handle it. She wasn't ready.

If only she'd acknowledged the depth of her feelings

for Buck before Julie had arrived. If only she'd told him she loved him. If only she knew he loved her, too.

There were a lot of *if onlys,* but only one reality, and she was facing that now. She wanted to bolt like a frightened filly.

As if Buck sensed her thoughts, he shifted toward the back door, casually leaning an elbow on the door frame, with what was definitely a half smile on his lips. Ellie glanced toward the living room, but Buck shook his head, cautioning her against that escape.

Resigned, Ellie shifted her gaze to Tyler. The boy was rocking on his feet in his excitement.

"You're glad to meet your mother, huh?" she asked gently, forcing an upward tilt to her lips, though she was under no illusion that it remotely resembled a smile.

Tyler's grin faltered, and he glanced anxiously at his father. "Dad?"

"It's okay, son," Buck reassured the boy. "Go ahead and tell her what you want to say."

Tyler was smiling again. "I'm—I'm not really all that happy to meet her," he said, but it was what he didn't say that gave Ellie her first tiny ray of hope.

Tyler hadn't called Julie his mother. At least not yet.

Still, Ellie was surprised by Tyler's words, especially given the past few minutes. "You're not?"

Tyler shook his head. "No. Not really."

"I guess I don't understand," said Ellie.

Tyler was looking edgy all of the sudden, and once again he glanced at his father for support.

Ellie brushed a lock of hair from the boy's forehead. "Don't worry, Tyler. You can tell me anything."

Buck stepped forward, laying his hands on Tyler's

shoulders. "Tyler and I have something we want to ask you," he said huskily, his look warm and gleaming.

Ellie's gaze widened on them both as Tyler nodded vigorously and Buck grinned.

"Dad wants to marry you," Tyler blurted suddenly. "You love him, right?"

Ellie was caught so off guard, she nearly fell over. Her knees felt like gelatin. Whatever she'd expected Tyler to say, this wasn't it.

She raised her eyes to Buck and saw the confirmation of love beaming from his gaze. He smiled and nodded.

Ellie wanted to answer, but the lump in her throat had grown to the size of a large boulder. Her heart pounded. As if a dam had burst, love welled in her heart for both of her men and sheer joy made her dizzy.

"How would you feel about staying around here forever?" she asked the boy.

Tyler's answering smile was more than adequate.

Buck leaned over the young man and planted a soft kiss on Ellie's lips. "I was hoping you'd say that."

"How could I refuse both of you?" she asked with a joyful laugh.

"Exactly," Buck agreed. "Why do you think I brought Tyler along with me? I didn't want to give you the chance to refuse."

Ellie reached her hands out, one hand brushing Buck's cheek and the other brushing Tyler's. Matching grins flashed back at her. Father and son.

Soon to be *her husband and son.*

"My two men," she murmured tenderly.

Tyler stepped out from between them, allowing Buck to pull Ellie close and kiss her again. Ellie was dizzy with delight and happier than she had ever been. Vaguely, she heard Tyler's voice from what seemed like a long distance.

"All right!"

With a secretive expression, Buck reached into the front pockets of his black jeans and then pulled out his hands, clenched in fists. "Pick a hand."

Ellie brushed her long hair back with her hand and then pointed at Buck's left fist. With a twinkle in his emerald green eyes, he opened his hand, but it was empty.

"Pick another hand," Buck suggested.

Tyler laughed in delight, and Ellie joined him.

Her heart roaring in her ears, Ellie took Buck's other hand and turned it over, pulling at his clamped fingers. Buck toyed with her a moment before opening his fist.

On the flat of his palm was an engagement ring, a simple gold setting with a sparkling solitaire. Ellie gasped, forgetting momentarily how to breathe.

"Oh, Buck. It's beautiful," she whispered as he slipped the ring on her left fourth finger.

"It was my mother's," he explained huskily. "I know she'd want you to have it."

"I'm sure she's smiling down from heaven right now," Ellie said, pressing a soft kiss to Buck's scratchy cheek. "I think she might have had this in mind all along."

Buck squeezed her hand and kissed her ring finger. "I imagine she did."

* * * * *

Dear Reader,

Babies should come with a warning label: Will Become Teenagers! My three teenage girls keep me hopping, and it is a great privilege to share with them the joys and sorrows of growing up, even if there is much pain involved. No one said being a parent was easy. When my children suffer, I suffer. Yet God has given me more blessings than I can count with my daughters, and I wouldn't have it any other way.

It was a beautiful journey for me to write a teenager into *His Texas Bride*. I loved every minute with Buck, Ellie and Tyler, and hope you do, as well.

I love to hear from my readers and try to respond personally to everyone. Please join my fan page on Facebook. I am on MySpace at: www.myspace.com/debkastner. You can also contact me directly by e-mail at DEBWRTR@aol.com. I look forward to hearing from you!

In Christ's love,

Deb Kastner

QUESTIONS FOR DISCUSSION

1. What made you pick up this book? Was it the cover? The author? The back cover copy?

2. In *His Texas Bride* Buck ran away from his problems instead of trying to work them out. Have you ever been in a situation from which you wanted to run? How did you deal with it?

3. Ellie had the rug pulled out from under her feet when Buck disappeared from her life, yet she moved on and focused on God. Relate an experience when you felt the "rug" was pulled out from underneath you. What did you do?

4. In the book Buck's ex-wife, Julie, chose to face those from whom she must ask forgiveness. Is this always the best course of action? Why or why not?

5. Why was it important for Buck and Tyler to forgive Julie? Have you ever struggled with this?

6. To which character in *His Texas Bride* do you most relate? Why?

7. What do you consider the prominent themes of *His Texas Bride?* How do they relate to your life?

8. Buck held on to his anger toward his mother until he'd almost forgotten why he was angry in the first

place. How does this happen, and how can you avoid having it happen to you? (See Ephesians 4:26)

9. Although Ellie considered her therapy ranch a Christian ministry, there is not much overtly Christian about what she does. Would you consider this a ministry? Why or why not?

10. Ellie was thrilled to watch Buck work with Morgan, a little girl with Down syndrome. Sometimes people find it uncomfortable or difficult to interact with those with physical or mental disabilities. Discuss your own experiences with people with disabilities.

11. Do you agree with Buck and Ellie's decision to let Tyler know Julie was his birth mother?

12. Have you ever acted rashly and then regretted it? What was the situation, and how did you handle it?

13. Because Ellie lost her parents, she had a very close relationship with Mama Esther. Is there anyone in your life who feels like true family even though they aren't blood relatives?

14. Have you ever lost sight of a hope or dream? How did you cope? Did you eventually see God's hand working in the situation? What hidden blessings did you find?

15. What will you remember most from this book? What lessons about love and faith did you learn?

*When his niece unexpectedly arrives at his
Montana ranch, Jules Parrish has no idea
what to do with her—or with Olivia Rose,
the pretty teacher who brought her.
Will they be able to build a life—
and family—together?*

*Here's a sneak peek of "Montana Rose"
by Cheryl St.John, one of the touching stories
in the new collection, TO BE A MOTHER,
available April 2010
from Love Inspired Historical.*

Jules Parrish squinted from beneath his hat brim,
certain the waves of heat were playing with his eyes.
Two females—one a woman, the other a child—stood
as he approached.

The woman walked toward him. Jules dismounted
and approached her. "What are you doing here?"

The woman stopped several feet away. "Mr. Parrish?"

"Yeah, who are you?"

"I'm Olivia Rose. I was an instructor at the
Hedward Girls Academy." She glanced back over her
shoulder at the girl who watched them. "My young
charge is Emily Sadler, the daughter of Meriel Sadler."

She had his attention now. He hadn't heard his
sister's name in years. *Meriel.*

"The academy was forced to close. I thought Emily

should be with family. You're the only family she has, so I brought her to you."

He took off his hat and raked his fingers through dark, wavy hair. "Lady, I spend every waking hour working horses and cows. I sleep in a one-room cabin. I don't know anything about kids—and especially not girls."

"What do you suggest?"

"I don't know. All I know is, she can't stay here."

*Will Olivia be able to change Jules's mind
and find a home for Emily—and herself?*

*Find out in
TO BE A MOTHER,
the heartwarming anthology from
Cheryl St.John and Ruth Axtell Morren,
available April 2010
only from Love Inspired Historical.*

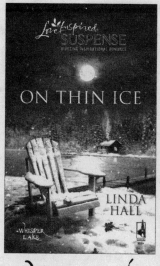

LARGER-PRINT BOOKS!

GET 2 FREE
LARGER-PRINT NOVELS
PLUS 2 FREE
MYSTERY GIFTS

Love Inspired

Larger-print novels are now available...

YES! Please send me 2 FREE LARGER-PRINT Love Inspired® novels and my 2 FREE mystery gifts (gifts are worth about $10). After receiving them, if I don't wish to receive any more books, I can return the shipping statement marked "cancel". If I don't cancel, I will receive 6 brand-new novels every month and be billed just $4.74 per book in the U.S. or $5.24 per book in Canada. That's a saving of over 20% off the cover price. It's quite a bargain! Shipping and handling is just 50¢ per book in the U.S. and 75¢ per book in Canada.* I understand that accepting the 2 free books and gifts places me under no obligation to buy anything. I can always return a shipment and cancel at any time. Even if I never buy another book, the two free books and gifts are mine to keep forever.

122 IDN E4KN 322 IDN E4KY

Name _____ (PLEASE PRINT) _____

Address _____ Apt. # _____

City _____ State/Prov. _____ Zip/Postal Code _____

Signature (if under 18, a parent or guardian must sign)

Mail to Steeple Hill Reader Service:
IN U.S.A.: P.O. Box 1867, Buffalo, NY 14240-1867
IN CANADA: P.O. Box 609, Fort Erie, Ontario L2A 5X3

**Are you a current subscriber to Love Inspired books
and want to receive the larger-print edition?
Call 1-800-873-8635 or visit www.morefreebooks.com.**

* Terms and prices subject to change without notice. Prices do not include applicable taxes. Sales tax applicable in N.Y. Canadian residents will be charged applicable provincial taxes and GST. Offer not valid in Quebec. This offer is limited to one order per household. All orders subject to approval. Credit or debit balances in a customer's account(s) may be offset by any other outstanding balance owed by or to the customer. Please allow 4 to 6 weeks for delivery. Offer available while quantities last.

Your Privacy: Steeple Hill Books is committed to protecting your privacy. Our Privacy Policy is available online at www.SteepleHill.com or upon request from the Reader Service. From time to time we make our lists of customers available to reputable third parties who may have a product or service of interest to you. If you would prefer we not share your name and address, please check here. ☐

Help us get it right—We strive for accurate, respectful and relevant communications. To clarify or modify your communication preferences, visit us at www.ReaderService.com/consumerschoice.

LILP10

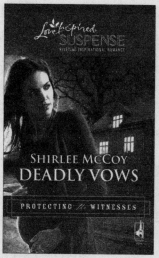

Love Inspired

TITLES AVAILABLE NEXT MONTH

Available March 30, 2010

A MOTHER'S GIFT
Arlene James and Kathryn Springer

LOVE LESSONS
Helping Hands Homeschooling
Margaret Daley

A FATHER FOR ZACH
Lighthouse Lane
Irene Hannon

HER FOREVER FAMILY
Mae Nunn

RODEO SWEETHEART
Betsy St. Amant

THE CINDERELLA LIST
Judy Baer

LICNMBPA0310